Life, Starring Me!

candy apple books...
just for you.
sweet. fresh. fun.
take a bite!

The Accidental Cheerleader by Mimi McCoy

The Boy Next Door by Laura Dower

Miss Popularity by Francesco Sedita

How to Be a Girly Girl in Just Ten Days
by Lisa Papademetriou

Drama Queen by Lara Bergen

The Babysitting Wars by Mimi McCoy

Totally Crushed by Eliza Willard

I've Got a Secret by Lara Bergen

Callie for President by Robin Wasserman

Making Waves by Randi Reisfeld and H.B. Gilmour

The Sister Switch
by Jane B. Mason and Sarah Hines Stephens

Accidentally Fabulous by Lisa Papademetriou

Confessions of a Bitter Secret Santa by Lara Bergen

Accidentally Famous by Lisa Papademetriou

Star-Crossed by Mimi McCoy

Accidentally Fooled by Lisa Papademetriou

Miss Popularity Goes Camping by Francesco Sedita

Life, Starring Me!

by Robin Wasserman

candy
apple

SCHOLASTIC INC.

New York Toronto London Auckland Sydney
Mexico City New Delhi Hong Kong Buenos Aires

For Barbara Blank and Jamie Feldman

The show couldn't have gone on without you.

ISBN-13: 978-0-545-10065-6
ISBN-10: 0-545-10065-8

12 11 10 9 8 7 6 5 4 3 2 1   9 10 11 12 13 14/0
40

Printed in the U.S.A.
First printing, May 2009

☆ Table of Contents ☆

Overture

You know those stories where some shy, mousy, ugly-duckling girl finds herself center stage, sweating it out under the spotlight? And everyone freaks out, thinking she's going to be a big flop, but she opens her mouth — and suddenly she's a hit? Then, after the encore and the standing ovation and the throwing roses at her feet, someone points to the girl and says, all shocked: "A star is born!"

This is not one of those stories.

I mean, I guess sometimes it happens that way. But not with me. I'm not "Surprise, a star is born!" material. I'm the opposite: I was *born* a star.

No, really. My dad took all these videos when I was little, and you can tell I wasn't just an ordinary kid, all red-faced and squealing. When I

1

squealed, people listened. Even then, I had *star presence.*

That's what my great-aunt Silva calls it. "You don't *learn* star presence," she always says. "You *live* it."

And that's what I've been doing my whole life.

Every star is a work in progress. By my thirteenth birthday, my progress had been straight up for thirteen years. Up like a skyscraper. Up like a rocket. Up like a shooting star.

Wait, you may be saying. *Shooting stars* go down. *They start in the sky, then flame out in the atmosphere and plummet toward the earth.*

Well, I was about to do the same thing.

I just didn't know it yet.

☆ *Chapter 1* ☆

Diva Rule #1: *"There are worse things than being called cute."*
— Kristin Chenoweth
(star of *You're a Good Man, Charlie Brown*)

"*Bon anniversaire, ma chérie,*" Great-aunt Silva said, leaning over to give me a kiss on each cheek. "That's French for happy birthday, my dear."

"I know," I said, even though I didn't. Pretty much the only French I knew was *oui* (yes), *non* (no), and *un croissant chocolat, s'il vous plaît* (a chocolate croissant, please). I guess some people might have learned more French after living in Paris for six weeks . . . but those people weren't starring in the international touring company of *Bye Bye Birdie*. I was.

Okay, it's not like the neon lights above the theater read BYE BYE BIRDIE STARRING RUBY DAY! But I had a very crucial part. A featured role. I played Randolph, the main character's little brother.

Yes, I was playing a boy.

3

So what? Like Great-aunt Silva says, vanity has no place in the theater. Even though I loved my long, thick, chestnut-colored hair, even though I'd been growing it out since I was seven years old, I knew the show was more important. So I cut it all off before the audition.

I got the part.

It wasn't my first big break. When I was six, I starred in my local theater's production of *Annie*. Then it was *Les Miserables*, at a big theater in Los Angeles, and after that, two national tours: *Mary Poppins* and *Gypsy*. I got *Bye Bye Birdie* when I was eleven, my first international tour. We hit Beijing, Barcelona, Buenos Aires — and those were just the B's. I'd visited almost fifteen countries — and I hadn't been home for more than a week at a time in two years.

That's where Great-aunt Silva comes in. My mom and dad had to stay back home in California with my little sister, Alana, so Great-aunt Silva came on the road with me. She homeschooled me in hotel rooms all over the world. She taught me how to say "yes" and "no" in thirteen languages. And most important, every day, no matter what, she got me to the theater on time.

"Through rain, sleet, flu, or yawn," she always says, "whatever it is, the show must go on."

And she should know.

Great-aunt Silva was an actress herself, forever ago. No, not just an actress — a diva. A *star*. She performed on Broadway until she got tired of staying in one place. ("I got too big for Broadway," she always says. "Or maybe Broadway got too small for me!") Great-aunt Silva never had any kids either. She says she wanted to fly free, like a bird without a nest.

"I simply cannot abide the little brats," she huffs, every time we get bumped off the sidewalk by a horde of kids coming home from school. "But you're different. Do you know why?"

I'm always ready with the answer she wants to hear. "Because I'm a star."

Then she laughs. "Not yet," she reminds me. "But we're working on it."

Great-aunt Silva hates the movies. "They're nothing but smoke and mirrors," she says. "A pale imitation of life. The stage *is* life."

And okay, in some ways, she's right. The stage is *my* life.

But when it comes to telling a good story — like, say, the story of me — sometimes movies can come in handy. If this were a movie, here's where I would stick the opening credits. (So make sure you picture my name coming first, in huge, hot-pink letters that fill up the whole screen.) Over the credits, I'd show a jumble of scenes of my six weeks in Paris, all mashed up together. Because that's what it feels like to be on tour — you're never sure what day it is or what time it is or sometimes even what country you're in. We'd been performing in Paris for six weeks, and in some ways, it felt like six minutes. In other ways, it felt like a lifetime.

So take a bunch of mixed and muddled memories, add some slo-mo, a spiffy song, and — don't forget — my name in lights, and you've got your opening credits montage:

Scene: There's me, Ruby Day, and the cast of *Bye Bye Birdie* performing a special concert in the giant cathedral of Notre Dame. An audience of almost 5,000. Our music echoing against stone ceilings that stretch up a hundred feet over our heads. Dappled light filtering through a 700-year-old stained-glass window.

Scene: A grand ball at the Louvre, Paris's most famous art museum, in honor of some famous French guy. Fancy dresses and fancier appetizers. The *Mona Lisa* hanging on the wall, giving us all her strange half smile like she's got some particularly juicy secret. A special performance of songs from

Les Miserables, featuring me, Ruby Day, singing my all-time favorite, "On My Own." (And singing it in French, which is harder than it looks. Trust me.)

Scene: International singing star (in training) Ruby Day, besieged by fans outside the theater's stage door. Signing program after program for a gaggle of shy, giggling girls. People see the crowd and get curious. "You someone famous?" they ask. I always shake my head no, but if Great-aunt Silva gets to them first, she tells them I'm a Swedish rock star or exiled Bulgarian royalty or the latest winner of *America's Next Hot Top Pop Star*. And when they get all excited and ask for my autograph, too, I put on a fake accent and sign a name for them. (*A* name, not my name. Often Penelope Pomplemousse, but sometimes I go with Stella Artichokie.)

Scene: "Lovely night for a moonlight picnic, Mademoiselle Pomplemousse," Great-aunt Silva says as she hops the low fence and clambers aboard the houseboat.

"You sure about this, Great-aunt Hildegard?" I ask, still standing on the edge of the Seine, looking doubtfully at the boat. Yes, it's the middle of the night and there's no one in sight. Yes, there's a picnic table and two chairs on the long, flat deck, perfect for eating *croissants chocolat* under the moonlight.

No, the boat doesn't belong to us.

"*Bien sur,* Penelope," Great-aunt Silva says, and she dangles the bag of croissants, knowing I can't resist.

I hop the fence.

Scene: The greatest night of not just my life, but *anyone's* life. Backstage passes to a special, private concert given by Patti LuPone, the greatest living Broadway diva. And not just backstage passes, not just a private audience with Patti LuPone herself, not just a handshake from the greatest living Broadway diva, but a *gift*.

Well, not really a gift — more like a sweaty old scarf that she was about to throw in the trash before Great-aunt Silva rescued it for me.

"That's kind of awesome," I say. "And kind of gross. It's totally soggy with sweat."

She looks at me like I'm nuts. "It's the sweat of a *genius*," she points out. Still, we carry it home in a plastic bag. Which works great until the wind blows the bag out of her hand, through the air . . . and into the river.

"The scarf!" I shriek.

Great-aunt Silva doesn't panic. She looks at me. She looks at the scarf, floating down the river. With a small shrug, she kicks off her shoes.

Then, even though it's December, she jumps in the river.

When they pull her out, looking like a drowned French sewer rat, she's shivering almost as hard as she's laughing — and she has the scarf wrapped around her left fist.

"Are you insane?" I hug her, even though now we both smell like dirty Seine water.

"It's *Patti LuPone*," she says, like I'm the crazy one because I didn't jump in. "What else was I supposed to do?"

End Scene.

Even a movie can only give you the highlights — the biggest, best, brightest moments. It glosses over all the little stuff in between, like the fresh crepes filled with hot, gooey Nutella; the window-shopping along the Boulevard Saint-Germain; trying on ridiculous feather covered dresses no one could ever afford. (And who would want to?) Not to mention the room service, the cast parties, the hours and hours of rehearsing, the performances, the standing ovations, and did I mention the autograph signing?

Okay, I know I mentioned the autograph signing, but I figured I'd mention it again because it was awesome.

Some things sound like they'd be really fun and exciting and glamorous, but when you actually do them, you find out they're about as exciting as a field trip to a wax factory.

But starring in the international touring production of *Bye Bye Birdie* wasn't as good as it sounds.

It was better.

There I was, spending my thirteenth birthday in Paris. And, since I had the day off, I was determined to spend it *in* Paris. We were leaving for Venice in another week, and I still hadn't done any of the normal touristy Paris things, like going to the top of the Eiffel Tower. "Normal is overrated," Great-aunt Silva always says, and I knew she was probably right. But that's what we were going to do on my birthday, whether Great-aunt Silva liked it or not. Just a normal afternoon . . . 900 feet off the ground.

"Jerry called while you were sleeping," Great-aunt Silva said that morning, before we could go anywhere. I was still in my pajamas, but she was already dressed for the day in a long, flowing Indian print skirt and a pink blouse that clashed with her bright orange (dyed) hair. "He wants to see you this morning. ASAP."

"Mmmf?" I mumbled around a bite of crumbly chocolate pastry.

She shrugged. "He didn't say why. Just that it was important."

I sighed. This always happened when I got a day off. There was some last-minute crisis — an emergency rehearsal, costume fittings, a dance lesson, publicity . . . annoying meetings with Jerry, the annoying producer.

"I'm sure it won't take long," Great-aunt Silva said. "We'll still have plenty of time for *la Tour Eiffel*." She puckered her magenta-stained lips into a frown. "Are you sure you don't want to invite any of your friends along? It is your birthday, after all."

I tried not to laugh. Friends? Where was I supposed to find any of those?

There was Thierry, the hotel doorman, who always winked at me when I came in at night still wearing my stage makeup. There was Alicia, the stagehand who traded cheesy magazines with me while we were killing time backstage. And, of course, there was Helen, the producer's hundred-year-old assistant, who was always pinching my cheeks and giving me used Dr. Seuss books soggy with her grandkids' drool.

Somehow I didn't think those were the kind of friends my great-aunt had in mind.

"My best friend is the stage," Great-aunt Silva always says.

My best friend — my only friend — was Great-aunt Silva.

The taxi dropped me outside the *Theatre de Grand Reves* just in time for my meeting with Jerry. The gleaming white buildings that lined the cobble-stone street looked pretty good for being 300 years old. Back home, the most ancient thing in town was the local strip mall, and that was built in the seventies. The *nineteen* seventies.

I swung open the door to Jerry's office, wondering what to expect.

"Ruby!" he boomed. When there were VIPs around, Jerry used his inside voice. But the rest of the time, he boomed pretty much everything. "Happy birthday!"

I perched on one of the chairs across from him, surprised that he'd remembered.

"You've been with us a long, long time, Ruby. How long has it been?"

"Two years," I said proudly. Almost none of the other cast members had been with the show for that long.

"This is an exciting time for someone like you — lots of new opportunities. You're not a little kid anymore, and you must be tired of people treating you like one."

Finally, someone had noticed.

Jerry leaned back in his chair and propped his arms behind his head. "You've definitely got that, that . . . certain something that can make you a star, Ruby. But you need to stretch your wings. Every little bird needs to leave the nest sometime and learn to fly, am I right?" He paused, and looked at me like he was waiting for an answer.

Only I had no idea what he was talking about. So I just nodded.

"Of course I'm right," he boomed even louder. "It's become clear to me that this part is a waste of your talents." He clapped a hand over his heart. "I'll tell you, it *pains* me to watch you confined by such a narrow role. A talent like yours deserves to shine. It's time for you to come out of the shadows, Ruby. You want something *better*. A new challenge. Right?"

Suddenly, like a cartoon lightning-bolt blast to my brain, I understood.

I was getting a promotion! Finally, someone had seen that I was too talented to play some shrimpy little brother. Jerry was offering me a new challenge — and that had to mean a new role. But which one?

I'd heard rumors that Cheryl Platz, the girl who starred as Kim McAfee (my "older sister" in the show), was jumping to a touring company of *Beauty and the Beast* in a couple months. Kim McAfee was a *lead* role. Did Jerry really think I was ready?

"Yes!" I cried. "You're right. I'm definitely ready for a new challenge."

"Great. Glad we're on the same page." Jerry stood up. He reached out to shake my hand, and squeezed tight. "It takes a lot of courage to leave the nest. But I have no doubt you're going to fly."

I was glowing.

Jerry sat down again and started flipping through some papers. A moment later he looked up and raised his eyebrows, like he was surprised I was still there.

"So, um, what happens next?" I asked.

"Talk to Helen on your way out." He flicked a hand like he was swatting bugs away from his face. "She'll have some stuff for you to fill out."

I practically floated out of his office. I couldn't wait to tell Great-aunt Silva. Forget the Eiffel Tower. There was no time to waste: I had a whole new part to learn. Happy birthday to me!

Helen's desk, just outside Jerry's office, looked like a tornado zone. There were papers, clipboards, pens, tissues, and candy wrappers strewn everywhere. The to-do pile towered so high you could only see her puffy gray bun poking over the top. I cleared my throat.

Helen looked up, and her eyes widened. "How are you doing, honey?"

"Great!"

"Oh." She looked kind of surprised. "Jerry did give you the talk, right? About how you're growing out of the part?"

I nodded.

"And you're . . . okay with it?"

It's like she thought I was some behind-the-scenes mouse with stage fright, instead of a star-in-training who'd been dreaming of this moment for my entire life. But then, this was the woman who thought I liked to read Dr. Seuss books in my spare time. *Soggy* Dr. Seuss books.

"I'm great with it," I assured her. "Jerry said there were some papers or something I have to fill out?"

"Yes, yes." She handed me a pen and a clipboard with a few forms attached. "All right here and waiting for you."

"So, when do I start?" I asked.

"Start what, dear?"

"The new part," I said. "Jerry didn't exactly say."

Helen closed her eyes for a moment and pressed her fingertips together. Then she looked up at me. "What exactly *did* Jerry say?"

I shrugged. "Just some stuff about how I was outgrowing my part, and how I had to take on a new challenge if I was going to be a star, and . . ."

Helen looked like she'd eaten a moldy *croissant chocolat.* And my stomach was starting to twist, like maybe I had, too.

She shook her head. "Ruby, dear . . . there is no new part. When Jerry starts talking like that, it only means one thing."

I had another lightning-bolt blast, but this time, it was the real thing. I was pretty sure I knew what she was going to say — so sure that I wanted to press my hands over my ears and sing every song I knew, loud enough to drown her out.

That's what I would have done if I were still a little kid. But I was thirteen years old. Old enough to stand there quietly and listen to Helen tell me what I already knew.

"You're fired."

16

☆ *Chapter 2* ☆

"Are you sure you won't come with me?" I asked, hoping I didn't sound too desperate.

Great-aunt Silva shook her head. "I served my time," she said, tapping a long, maroon nail against my plane ticket. "When I left that town thirty years ago, I promised myself I wouldn't be back for a long, long while."

My dad grew up in Alencia, California, just like Great-aunt Silva (she's his mom's older sister). But unlike Great-aunt Silva, he never left. I don't know why. Alencia's about an hour outside of Los Angeles and has nothing but strip malls, car dealerships, and fast-food restaurants. Not the kind of place anyone sane would choose to live. But my plane was due to land there at 6:30 P.M.

It was a one-way ticket.

I slumped down in the hard plastic airport seat and watched the clock on the departures screen tick down the minutes. Fourteen more to go before I would leave my whole life behind and wing my way back to Nowheresville.

I stuffed the last bite of my croissant into my mouth, swallowing it even though it tasted like cardboard. I'd hoped for one last taste of Paris, but it tasted more like the kind of thing you'd buy at some store called Le Good Food in the Alencia mall. I should have known better — you can't get anything real in an airport.

"You must be eager to see your parents and your sister," Great-aunt Silva said. She sat on the very edge of her seat, like she didn't want to touch any more of it than necessary.

"I see them all the time," I muttered. Well, maybe not all the time, but some holidays, and a couple weeks every summer. Afterward, I was always sad for a few days — seeing them made me remember how much I missed them. Usually I tried not to think about it, because other-wise, I got too homesick. But now I kind of wanted to throw up at the thought of going home for good.

"Maybe if I talk to Jerry again?" I was definitely

sounding desperate. "I could make him see that I'm not too big. I can slouch!"

Great-aunt Silva clucked her tongue against the roof of her mouth. "What do I always tell you about the land of fantasy?"

"It's a nice place to visit, but you wouldn't want to live there," I recited dutifully. I knew she was right. (That's what was so annoying.) Jerry had already hired someone else to take my place, a disgustingly adorable ten-year-old from Mississippi. A ten-year-old *boy*.

"Don't look so glum," Great-aunt Silva said. "Every star needs to have *life experiences*. Before you can get up onstage and pretend to be someone else, you have to know what it's like to be yourself."

"But I'm *having* life experiences," I pointed out. "Or at least I was, before Jerry fired me. What about the time we got locked out of the hotel room in Hong Kong? Or when we snuck into that tapestry room in Buckingham Palace? Or when I did that duet with the crown prince of Bulgaria? Don't any of those count?"

"Of course they do," she allowed. "But what if one day you want to audition for a role as a 'normal' seventh grader?"

I snorted again. "Why would anyone ever write a show about that?"

Great-aunt Silva shook her head. "I wasn't suggesting that you *be* a normal seventh grader. I was suggesting you practice *acting* like one. You know what I always say — a great star truly lives her role."

"I guess."

I gave Great-aunt Silva a tight hug. She smelled like Paris. "I'm going to miss you," I whispered into her neck. "I'll miss all of it."

"Use it," she whispered back.

"What?"

"Whatever you're feeling, *feel* it as deeply as possible, and file it away in your brain. Life experiences, remember?"

"I'll remember," I promised her, even though I wasn't quite sure what she was talking about. "And I'll try to . . . feel deeply. Or whatever."

"I have no doubt you will." Great-aunt Silva grinned and raised her eyebrows. "Or whatever."

Home. Or another airport, about 6,000 miles closer to home. Let me set the stage: One escalator, one customs checkpoint, and 300 miserable jet-lagged passengers fresh off the plane, every single one of them gawking at the crazy lady in baggage claim

20

shrieking, "Rebecca! Rebecca!" at the top of her lungs.

And starring in the role of Crazy Shouting Lady? My mom.

She wrapped her arms around me and squeezed so tight I could barely breathe. I closed my eyes. A warm, happy feeling gushed through me, and everything I'd been worried about disappeared. For about fifteen seconds.

"It's Ruby," I reminded her, stepping back. My dad was already pulling my suitcases off the baggage carousel. He lugged them over to us, then scooped me into a bear hug.

"Funny, I have a distinct memory of naming you Rebecca," my mother teased. Even without looking, I could hear the smile in her voice. "And I could have sworn I was there when you were born."

"Well, in all fairness, Becca was there, too," my father pointed out. "Though I doubt she remembers it quite as vividly as we do."

"I don't know, you guys are getting pretty old," I joked. "Maybe your memories are fading."

My mom laughed. "You're right — for all I know, we named you Gertrude. Maybe we should just start calling you that."

"Or Trudie," my father suggested. "Since you hate the name Rebecca so much."

"How can we ever make it up to you?" my mother asked, pouring on the fake guilt. "Giving you such a horrendous name to bear through your life?"

"Come on, you know that's not it," I protested. There was nothing *wrong* with the name Rebecca Davenstein. It just wasn't . . . me. "Ruby Day" had so much more star presence. I've never understood why a person should have to walk around with some name that their parents picked out before they were even born, anyway. Lucky for me, my parents let me be whoever I wanted to be, even if I wanted to be Ruby Day.

But they never stopped teasing me about it.

"So where's the little princess?" I asked. That would be my sister, Alana. Back when I lived at home, she was obsessed with this princess costume she had. She wore the cheesy plastic tiara everywhere, even to kindergarten. After I went on tour, she grew out of it, but I wasn't about to let her forget. Wasn't that what big sisters were for?

My parents gave each other a look. "Waiting in the car."

That was weird. Usually when I came home for a visit, Alana was the first person to spot me getting off the plane. She would shriek my name and run across the terminal, launching herself at me like a grinning, curly-haired rocket. It was hideously embarrassing.

But also kind of sweet.

I hadn't seen her in almost nine months. The last time I came home, she was off on some school trip, and the time before that, she was visiting our grandparents in Oregon. It was so weird to think that my twerpy, tiara-wearing baby sister was old enough to go places on her own. Then again, she was eleven years old. When I was that age, I was living in Beijing and learning how to say "No thank you, I don't eat pig intestines" in Chinese.

There was someone waiting for us in the car all right, but it wasn't Alana. At least, not the Alana I remembered. Last time I saw my sister, she'd been wearing a paint-streaked sweatshirt two sizes too big and an old flowered skirt from the back of our mom's closet. Her wild hair had looked like the tangle of dirty ropes at the business end of a mop, and her mouth was constantly turned up in a gap-toothed smile.

This new Alana had her gloss-slathered lips pressed tightly together in a thin frown. Her hair was straight and shiny, falling neatly just below

her shoulders. There wasn't a smudge of paint —
or anything else — on her stylish white shirt or
perfectly cut jeans.

"*Bonjour*, princess," I said, slipping into the
backseat.

The creature sitting next to me didn't respond.
Arms crossed, back rigid, she stared straight
ahead.

As we drove back to the house, my parents
chattered about all the things we could do together
now that I was home, but I barely listened. I
couldn't stop staring at my little sister and waiting
for her to talk to me. Or to do *something* that
would prove that aliens hadn't taken over her
brain while I was away.

But she didn't speak, not for the whole ride
home. When we finally pulled into the driveway,
she jumped out as soon as the car stopped moving. "Trina's mom is picking me up in twenty
minutes," she said to Mom.

"I think your cleats are still upstairs," my mom
called as Alana ran into the house.

"Cleats?" I asked.

"Alana's a starting forward on her soccer
team," my dad said proudly.

Sports? My little sister — the one who once
threw a temper tantrum when a teacher wouldn't

let her play T-ball in her princess dress — played a *sport*?

On purpose?

Maybe I'm dreaming, I thought. Maybe I'm going to wake up and it's going to be my birthday morning, and everything's going to go back to the way it used to be. It didn't seem likely.

But I gave myself a good, hard pinch, just in case.

The scene: Family dinner number one, *chez Davenstein* (that's French for "house of mind-numbing boredom"). Stage left, a tiled kitchen counter piled high with all the dirty pots and pans required to make my dad's lasagna, which was my favorite food when I was nine. Stage right, a wall of framed family photos. I'm not in most of them. And center stage, the family Davenstein sitting down to dinner — except Alana, who is off playing soccer somewhere. For some reason.

The characters: Mark Davenstein, playing The Dad. Melina Martinez Davenstein as The Mom. And starring me, as The Daughter Who's Ready to Go Back to Paris.

Let's say you were putting on a musical about my family and you wanted to cast actors to play my parents. For my dad, you'd want someone not too tall and not too short, with glasses and a bald spot on the top of his head that was big enough to fit a smiley face drawn with black permanent marker. I know this for a fact. (I got grounded for a week; the smiley face lasted for two.)

For my mom, you'd need an actress with curly black hair, flashing eyes, and a lopsided smile that always looked like she was trying not to laugh. Also, you'd want an actress who could act like a terrible cook. (When people find out I'm half Mexican-American, they always think that means I speak Spanish and eat a lot of homemade Mexican food. But my mom grew up in San Francisco, speaking English from day one, and the only thing she knows how to cook is grilled cheese. And by "cook," I mean "burn.")

If life were a musical, this scene would be set to a song called "Lasagna Blues." With lines like "Dad thought this was what I'd want / But I just miss my chocolate croissant. / I got the lasagna blues." (If it were a Disney musical, that's where the lasagna would start singing and dancing along: "I'm so tasty / Please don't waste me!")

Life wasn't a musical, not anymore. But I had a plan to fix that.

"I was reading *Variety* on the plane," I told my parents. "I've already found a bunch of shows that are auditioning in LA next week. Can one of you give me a ride into the city?"

My mom raised her eyebrows. "Auditions? For what?"

"For a new show." Didn't I just say that? "Like Great-aunt Silva always says —"

"You just got home," my father cut in, rolling his eyes like he always did when I mentioned my great aunt. "What's your hurry?"

"Showbiz never takes a vacation," I said. That was another Great-aunt Silva quote, but I knew better than to say so. "Anyway, there's a national touring company of *Gypsy* that's auditioning in LA on Wednesday, so I was thinking —"

"Wednesday's a school day," my mother said. "So that's not going to work."

I froze. "Um, did you say *school*?"

"Did you somehow manage to skip six grades and graduate from high school while you were over there in Paris?" my mom asked.

I just stared at her.

"Didn't think so," she said. "So, *school*. What did you think you'd be doing?"

I hadn't been to a normal school in years. Great-aunt Silva taught me most of the time, though sometimes there were tutors. But it was always one-on-one, on my schedule and my terms.

27

That was so much more civilized than the thought of — I shuddered — *middle school*. "It's kind of silly for me to start school, don't you think?" I pointed out. "I'll probably get another part in a couple weeks and then I'll just have to leave again."

My father opened his mouth, then closed it again. He looked at my mother. "Do you want to tell her?"

"Not particularly," she said.

"Well, *I* don't want to tell her," he said. "Rock, paper, scissors for it?"

"Would you guys stop joking around and just *tell* me?" I burst out.

My mom gave me a big, fake smile. "Your father and I think it would be good for you to spend a little more time at home."

"Define 'little.'"

"Well . . . no one's saying you have to live here for the rest of your life," my mom said.

"*No one's* saying that," my dad repeated with a grin. "You've got to move out eventually — how else am I going to get that game room I've always wanted?"

My mom shot him her no-joking-for-the-next-five-minutes look. "We're not talking about forever," she said. "Just the rest of the year."

Excuse me?

"It's January," I pointed out. "That's *months*! What about my career?"

"You're thirteen years old," my mother said. "What's your hurry?"

She didn't understand. She never had. Great-aunt Silva says that there are two kinds of people in this world: stars, and everyone else. Mom and Dad were definitely "everyone else."

"Your career will still be here at the end of the school year," my father said. "But seventh grade won't be. Your mother and I just want you to spend some time as a normal kid. Going to school, coming home to your family every night. Normal."

"Normal is overrated," I muttered.

Then I laid down my fork, even though most of my lasagna and two soggy pieces of garlic bread were still on my plate. "I'm going to my room."

"Dearest child of mine," my mother said in her I'm-sort-of-teasing-but-not-really voice. "When you were on tour, where did you eat dinner?"

I shrugged. "In the hotel suite, usually. Room service."

"And what did you do with your plate when you were done?" she asked.

What did it matter? "We put them outside the

29

room, I guess. Someone took them away overnight."

My dad handed me his plate. He'd taken three helpings of lasagna and eaten every bite. "Step one of being a normal kid," he said. "Clear the table."

"Step two —" My mom pointed to the sink, piled high with pots and pans. "Sunday is your night to do the dishes."

I didn't even know *how* to do the dishes. No one had asked me to do a chore in four years. "But —"

I must have looked even more clueless than I felt, because my parents started laughing. My mom tossed me a bottle of liquid detergent and handed me a scrub brush. "Welcome home, Rebecca."

I'm not Rebecca, I almost said. *I'm Ruby.* But for the first time in a long while, it didn't feel true. After all, I couldn't quite picture international singing and acting sensation Ruby Day doing the dishes.

Rebecca Davenstein, on the other hand, pushed up her sleeves, plunged her hands into the soapy water, and got to work.

Chapter 3

Life experiences, I reminded myself, standing outside the door of Alencia Valley Middle School. *Every star needs life experiences.*

I reminded myself that it was only for a few months. Then I could go back on the road.

I reminded myself that I'd made it through five years of elementary school, and they hadn't been so bad.

I reminded myself that I'd found my way around some of the biggest cities in the world all on my own. I could handle middle school.

I reminded myself that it didn't matter that Alana was back at Millview Elementary, because I certainly didn't need my little sister — my bratty, sullen little sister who didn't even like me anymore — to show me around.

I reminded myself that I was an actress — how hard could it be to act like a normal seventh grader?

Then I ran out of things to remind myself. I took a deep breath.

And stepped inside.

You know how people always say, "It was like a zoo"? In a zoo, the wild animals are locked away in cages. In a zoo, you're safe — at least as long as you're human.

Alencia Valley Middle School was *not* like a zoo.

The noise hit me first. Hundreds of kids all talking and shouting and laughing at the same time.

Then there was the smell. Once, in Paris, a bunch of us in the cast took a tour of the sewer system. (*Not* my idea.) They led us through the damp, sludgy tunnels, with dirty water dripping on our heads and the stink of mold and rats and you-don't-want-to-know-what-else drifting up into our faces.

Alencia Valley Middle School smelled slightly worse than that.

The bell rang, and the cageless zoo of middle schoolers turned into a stampede. Hundreds of bodies flowed toward me, sweeping me down toward the stairway at the end of the hall. I pressed myself against a bank of lockers and squeezed my eyes shut.

I handled the Beijing subway system, I reminded myself. I can handle this.

A moment later, the flood had passed, the hallway was empty — and I had no idea where I was supposed to go. I wandered down the hall, hating how helpless I felt. That's when I spotted the poster. It was bright purple, with a familiar word written across the top in thick, black letters: AUDITION!

AUDITIONS FOR THE WINTER MUSICAL WILL BE HELD JANUARY 12, 13, AND 14, the poster said. That was a week ago. I'd missed them. But who cared? I was a pro. The drama kids would probably beg me to be in the show. A line of small print ran along the bottom of the poster: ANY QUESTIONS, SEE MS. HEDLEY, ROOM S12. I decided I would go see her right after school.

Having a plan was a little like having a script, and that made me feel a lot less helpless. Maybe I could actually figure out a way to make this whole middle school thing work.

At least until I went back on the road again.

*   *   *

I didn't learn much algebra that day, or much earth science, or history, but I did manage to learn:

1. To open your locker, spin the dial three times to the right, two times to the left, then once to the right. Memorize your combination, because if you write it down on a piece of paper, and then *lose* that piece of paper, everyone in sight will stand there laughing at you while you try a million numbers at random and then have to go down to the office and get someone to give you the combination again.

2. Talking to someone you don't know is a bad idea. If you *have* that bad idea, you probably shouldn't pick the captain of the girls' field hockey team who dresses like she's on her way to a photo shoot for *Teen Chic Magazine*. And if you do pick her, you probably shouldn't start the conversation by helpfully telling her that her fly's down.

3. Don't use the south stairwell, because it's stink bomb central.

4. Don't stop on the middle stairwell on the way to lunch to tie your shoes, unless you want some kid on the second level to pour his

carton of chocolate milk all over your new
purple sequined sweater. Not to mention turn
your irreplaceable formerly-owned-by-Patti-
LuPone scarf into a soggy brown mess.

5. Whatever you do, don't, don't, *don't* sit down
at a random table in the cafeteria next to
people you remember from fourth grade and
expect to polish the good old days of *then* into
some bright and shiny *now*.

In the movies, cafeterias are easy. One glance
is all you need to tell who everyone is and where
you belong. The nerds sit at one table, comparing
pocket protectors; next, the jocks, with their mus-
cles and their cheerleaders; the Prada patrol,
wannabe fashion queens who wouldn't know Paris
couture if they tripped over it on their way to
the mall; art freaks streaked with paint; and, of
course, the drama kids, dressed in black, quot-
ing Shakespeare, and breaking into song when
inspired by an especially tasty plate of meat loaf.
My people.

That's in the movies. But the kids in this cafeteria all dressed alike — girls in tank tops, hoodies,
and fitted jeans; guys in oversized T-shirts and
baggy jeans. (Other than my chocolate milk-

soaked disaster, not a sequin or feather in sight.) Some of them had probably been in my morning classes, but I'd been too busy staring at the school map to memorize anyone's face. But suddenly, I spotted them, buried in the crowd — people I actually recognized.

"Jenna?" I said, hurrying over to the table where the familiar blond girl nibbled at a sandwich. In fourth grade, Jenna Peters, Andrea Leach, and I used to hang out all the time. We played hopscotch on the blacktop and had contests on the swings to see who could touch the tree branches with our toes. These days, Jenna was a little taller and a lot shinier (shiny blond hair, shiny pink lips, shiny silver sneakers), but I was pretty sure it was her. "Jenna, it's me. Ruby. Remember? Can I sit with you guys?"

Jenna barely looked up.

"Rebecca Davenstein," I added helpfully, in case she didn't remember that I'd renamed myself Ruby Day. "We used to —"

"Oh, I remember Rebecca," another girl at the table said, rolling her eyes. Her dark red hair was pulled back in a loose ponytail and her eyebrows were plucked almost bare. I took a closer look. Was that *Andrea*? Quiet, shy Andrea, who followed me around and did whatever I told her to, even if

36

it got her grounded? (It only happened that one time, I swear.) "Wasn't she that stuck-up girl who always thought she was going to be famous?"

Jenna smirked. "You mean the one who missed your piano recital because she had an audition?"

"Yeah," Andrea said. "The one who skipped your birthday party because she had an audition."

Jenna took a sip of her vitaminwater. "And didn't she ditch out on that big presentation we did, the one that was worth, like, half of our grade, because she —"

"Had an audition," Andrea finished. "Yeah, I heard she was back in town. She totally flamed out or something. Forgot her lines and ruined the whole show."

You're such a liar! I wanted to shout, but I was frozen.

"*I* heard she got homesick and started crying onstage, right in the middle of her big solo," said some other girl I didn't even know.

Liar! I thought again. But even though I'd been performing since I was three years old and I'd never had a moment of stage fright, I couldn't make myself open my mouth.

Andrea shrugged. "Maybe they just fired her because she wasn't very good."

Liar, I thought. But what if she wasn't?

Wasn't that what I'd been secretly thinking? People who were destined to be stars didn't get fired. They didn't get "too old" for the part — or if they did, they got a better one. But here I was, without a part at all.

Except the part of Ruby Day, middle school loser.

Jenna glanced up at me, pretending like she'd just noticed I was there. "Oh my gosh!" She widened her eyes. "Rebecca — oh, I mean, Ruby? Is that you? It's so *awesome* to see you again! What happened to the whole big star thing?" She elbowed Andrea.

"Yeah, are you back here for some kind of big show?" Andrea asked, giggling. "Can we still buy tickets?"

"I have to, uh . . ." I started inching away. The room was getting blurry. Not because I was starting to cry. I'd stood up to crazy directors, jerky choreographers, angry critics — it took more than a couple ex-friends to make me cry. Blurry eyes or not. "Excuse me. I have to. Go."

I ran out of the cafeteria, pretending I was going to find the bathroom. But I didn't. Instead, I hid in the empty middle stairwell. I stood next to the railing, staring down at the concrete stairs, trying to pretend I was anywhere else. I closed my eyes and imagined that I was standing against the railing of the Pont des Arts, with the Seine flowing beneath me and the church bells ringing in the background. And it was working — so well that I barely noticed the *real* bell ringing or the kids flooding into the stairwell. I didn't notice anything until, just below me, someone screamed.

I opened my eyes. Then — when it was way too late — I noticed three very important things:

1. Two guys stood next to me along the railing, pointing at me and mouthing, "It was her!"
2. Two chocolate milk containers were perched on the railing next to me.
3. At the bottom of the stairs, a very wet, very angry girl shrieked as chocolate milk dripped down her curly red hair. "Look what you did!" she screeched. At *me*.

"It wasn't me!" I called as she disappeared into the crowd. "I swear!"

But she was already gone.

As soon as the final bell rang, I hurried down to the basement level to find Ms. Hedley and ask her about joining the school musical. Room S12 was empty, but I could hear muffled voices coming from behind a set of big wooden doors. I pushed my way through and found myself in the auditorium. It was totally dark, except for a single wide spotlight that shined on a group of kids sitting in a circle onstage.

Even though I wanted to run, I forced myself to walk up slowly to the circle of kids. I loved the way the wooden slats felt beneath my feet, and the way the chairs in the auditorium disappeared in the spotlight's shadow. I could imagine an audience out there, watching my every move.

Now that I'm back where I belong, everything's going to be fine, I told myself.

"You!" someone said angrily. It was chocolate milk girl. Uh-oh.

"Look, I'm sorry," I said quickly. "You were gone before I could explain that it wasn't —"

"This is a private rehearsal, cast members only," she snapped. "Just in case you've suffered some kind of mental meltdown, here's a reminder: The cast does not include *you*."

I'd spent all day keeping my mouth shut, and I was tired of it. The theater was *my* turf, and I wasn't afraid of looking dumb anymore.

"Maybe it *didn't* include me," I retorted. "But lucky for you, it does now."

The girl stood up. "I'm president of the drama club, which means I'm in charge here, and I say you have to go. *Now*."

A middle-aged woman with long, flowing blond hair and a loose purple shirtdress stood up and patted the girl's shoulder. "Actually, Maureen dear, *I'm* in charge here. Although, of course, when we speak of the *theater*—" She said it in a weird accent, drawing the word out into three long syllables, like thee-ate-or. "—only our *feelings* are in charge. Isn't that right, everyone?"

The other kids mumbled and nodded. I could tell they were thinking exactly what I was: This woman was a total flake.

Still, she was a total flake who sounded like she might be on my side.

The woman—I figured it was Ms. Hedley—turned toward me. "Now, what is it I can do for you, Ms. . . . ?"

"Day," I said. "Ruby Day. And you want me in your cast."

"Well, Ruby Day, I'm afraid you missed the auditions—"

"I'm new," I said confidently. Once she heard me sing, she wouldn't care whether I'd missed the auditions or not. "I've been on tour with the international company of *Bye Bye Birdie*."

41

I know it sounds like I was bragging, but up onstage, it's not called bragging — it's called getting the part.

Judging from the expressions on the other kids' faces, they didn't quite see the difference.

The teacher's hands fluttered to her heart. "Oh my, a *thespian*!" She turned to the group of kids and clapped loudly. "Cast members, a true thespian walks among us!"

Whatever she was waiting for, it didn't happen. The kids just stared. Someone snickered.

"Tell me, Ruby Day, what kind of experience do you have with our fair muse — by which I mean," she added in a stage whisper, "the theater."

Lucky for me, I had a copy of my résumé and headshot right in my bag. Well, it wasn't exactly *luck* — I carry them with me everywhere. I handed them over to Ms. Hedley, so she could see exactly why she needed me in her show.

"Ms. Hedley, we already cast all the parts," the girl named Maureen complained. "There's no room left."

"There's always room for a true *thespian*," Ms. Hedley told her.

"But that's not fair —"

"Maureen!" Ms. Hedley said it sweetly and softly, but she got her point across. Maureen shut her mouth. "Maureen's right," Ms. Hedley continued. "We have cast all the parts in *Monster Mash: The Musical. . . .*"

A hollow spot opened up in my throat. I swallowed hard.

"But given all your *professional* experience, I'm sure we can make room for you."

Something huge and heavy lifted off my shoulders. I was going to be a star again, even if it meant performing in this tiny auditorium, in this lame town, in this amateur show. Even if it meant sharing the stage with this girl Maureen. For the first time, I began to think things would be okay.

Until Ms. Hedley said those four terrifying little words:

"Welcome to the chorus."

Chapter 4

Diva rule #4: *"You've gotta be original, because if you're like someone else, what do they need you for?"*

— Bernadette Peters
(star of *Into the Woods*)

A typical day on the road with a professional, Broadway-caliber, international touring company:

Wake up at seven A.M. Leave dirty clothes outside hotel suite for maid to launder. Stop at local *boulangerie* for a fresh-baked croissant, hot out of the oven, so warm and buttery it almost melts on your tongue.

Nine to ten A.M.: voice lesson.

Ten A.M. to noon: Dance lesson (modern jazz on Mondays and Wednesdays, tap on Tuesdays and Thursdays).

Noon to one P.M.: Quick break for lunch (a fresh-made tomato mozzarella baguette if I was lucky, a frozen quiche heated up in the theater microwave if I wasn't).

One P.M.: Last-minute rehearsal to go over new choreography.

Three to seven P.M.: Tutoring.

Seven to seven forty-five P.M.: Warm-up, costuming, makeup, crazed running around backstage to get everything done on time.

Seven forty-five P.M.: VIP meet and greets.

Eight P.M.: Curtain up!

Out of the theater, back to the hotel, and in bed by eleven forty-five (even though the rest of the cast was out on the town doing whatever it is I wasn't allowed to do). And up again the next morning to do it all over again.

See, it's not like I was on vacation all that time — it was a lot of work. Hard work. The kind that calluses your feet and bruises your knees and strains your voice and drives you insane, all while you have to stare into the spotlight and smile, pretending that you're loving every minute of it.

Except I never had to pretend.

A typical day *chez Davenstein*: Wake up at seven A.M. Gulp down disgusting generic oat cereal that my parents insist on buying because it's cheaper than the brand-name stuff. Ask Alana for something — salt, juice, green shirt that looks suspiciously similar to the green shirt that disappeared from my closet — and get ignored.

Seven forty-five A.M.: Climb onto school bus and take the empty seat right behind the driver. Pretend not to notice that everyone's ignoring me, because that's better than the first few days, when they tossed spitballs into my hair.

Eight-twenty A.M. to three P.M.: School. (One word: *ugh*.)

After school, there was rehearsal. Then home again, where I was treated like a servant. I had to wash my own clothes! Do my own dishes! Clean my own room!

I felt like Cinderella. And okay, so my ugly stepsister-who-was-actually-my-not-particularly-ugly-real-sister-even-if-she-pretended-we-didn't-know-each-other had to do plenty of chores, too, but she didn't seem to care. I didn't know how she could stand it.

I couldn't stand anything. Not the gross food, not the boring teachers, and definitely not the dishes.

Rehearsals for *Monster Mash: The Musical* should have been the bright spot in every cloudy day. And maybe they would have been, if it weren't for flaky Ms. Hedley and her loyal minion Maureen.

Ms. Hedley acted like she was born onstage, but I was pretty sure she was a total poseur. Her staging was awkward and her choreography was ridiculous. Not to mention the fact that she wouldn't stop talking about her actor husband, Dash Hedley, like he was supposed to be the Next Big Thing — even though the rumor was that he worked in the kitchen at the Chili Shack, where they let him perform his one-man show as dinner theater on Sunday nights.

The show itself was okay, I guess. I liked the music, and the story was kind of funny. Basically, *Monster Mash* was about a monster war, vampires vs. zombies vs. werewolves, except instead of killing each other, the monsters sang and danced. At least until a beautiful young maiden — played by Maureen, of course — brought peace to the monster kingdom and they all lived happily ever after. Or as happy as you can get when you're the living undead, shuffling around eating brains or drinking blood or sprouting nose hair every time there's a full moon. The other kids weren't, you know, star quality, but most of them weren't bad. I knew that if Ms. Hedley would just listen to my advice, we could probably put on a pretty awesome show.

But Ms. Hedley wasn't interested.

"Don't you think it would be better if the zombies entered from stage right?" I asked her at my first rehearsal.

"Yours is not to think," she said in that airy, sweet voice. "Yours is to *act*."

"We had a crowd scene in *Bye Bye Birdie*, too," I told her a few minutes later, "and everyone was bumping into each other, just like this, until the choreographer came up with this idea to —"

"Every show presents its own unique trials and tribulations," she said, "and it's our job to confront those in the present, not the past."

Then, later: "Maybe if we shift the key of Maureen's solo, she'll be able to hit the high notes?" I suggested. "We did something like that for the girl playing Kim in —"

"Thank you, Ruby dear," Ms. Hedley said. "We're so lucky to have such a precious resource of theatrical knowledge." Then she turned her back on me. Message: *Thanks, but no thanks.*

"Maureen, is your throat getting sore?" a girl with sleek blond braids asked eagerly. "Can I get you something to drink?"

"How about some tea?" added a girl dressed almost exactly the same, but with brown braids. "We can snag some from the teacher's lounge."

"Perfect," Maureen said without looking at

them. She launched into her solo again. The girls scurried away, shooting identical glares at me as they passed.

This time, before Maureen's voice could crack, she forgot one of her lines.

"You know, in *Bye Bye Birdie*, we stayed on book until everyone was pretty much perfect, so we didn't have to worry about —"

Ms. Hedley sighed loudly. "Ruby, perhaps you could share your wisdom with fellow members of the chorus while darling Maureen and I work through this song?"

"Translation: Stop bugging us and go hang out with the tone-deaf klutzes, where you belong," Maureen whispered, quietly enough that Ms. Hedley couldn't hear.

So much for being helpful.

"Maureen's such a *darling*, isn't she?" someone murmured as I slumped down in a seat near the edge of the stage with the rest of the chorus.

I snorted.

"Kayla Wang," the girl sitting next to me said, smiling. I'd seen her in a couple of my classes. She was short, with shoulder-length black hair that was tied back with a brightly colored scarf. "Tone-deaf klutz." She held out her hand.

I shook it. "Ruby Day. I'm new here. I —"

"Oh, I know!" she said. "You've been on tour. *Bye Bye Birdie*, and before that, *Les Miz*, and —" She blushed. "I, uh, snuck a look at your résumé. You know, the one you gave to Ms. Hedley? I couldn't resist. Is that weird?" She answered herself before I could. "Okay, it's a little weird, but then, *I'm* a little weird, so that makes sense."

"It's not that weird," I assured her. "But why do you care?"

"Are you *kidding* me?" Her eyes bugged out. "Can we discuss how exciting your life has been, compared to those of us unlucky enough to be stuck here? The black hole of hideous nothingness known as Alencia, California?" She winced as, up onstage, Maureen's voice cracked on a high note. "You'd probably do anything to be out on the road again, right?"

I shrugged. Of course I would, but I didn't want to admit it to a total stranger. Especially since I was kind of embarrassed about the whole getting fired thing. "Being home for a while isn't so bad," I told her. "And being in *Monster Mash* will be . . . uh . . . fun."

Kayla gave me a friendly shrug. "Yeah, right. I'm sure you *love* being in the chorus while Velma Kelly over there hogs the spotlight."

"Velma Kelly?"

"You know, like in *Chicago*?" Kayla prompted. "The obnoxious diva who doesn't care about anything but being a star?"

"No, I know who she is, I'm just —"

"Surprised that *I* know?" Kayla raised her eyebrows. "Did you think you were the only one around here who knew anything about musicals?"

Well . . . *yes*.

"No," I lied. "But most kids our age who like musicals are all about *The Lion King* or something, you know?"

Kayla rolled her eyes. "Oh, trust me, I know." She shook her head. "Can we discuss how much Elton John makes me want to vomit? And don't even get me started on Stephen Schwartz. It's like, hello, you wrote *Godspell*! And now all of a sudden, *Wicked* is the best thing you can come up with? Is it really necessary for every song to sound. *Exactly. The. Same*?"

I decided not to mention that I loved *Wicked*. I didn't want to ruin the first interesting conversation I'd had in a week.

"So you're really into this stuff?" I asked.

"Why else would I subject myself to this every year?" Kayla spread her arms toward the stage and shook her head. "I mean, I guess I can't really talk, since I have *zero* talent. A real director probably wouldn't even let me in the show. Lucky for me, Ms. Hedley's not quite . . . Broadway-caliber."

"One more time, Maureen darling," Ms. Hedley told her star just then. She glanced toward the chorus. "The rest of you, get ready for the Circle of Energy!"

Kayla and I groaned in harmony.

At the beginning of the rehearsal, Ms. Hedley had made us all sit in a big circle onstage and clasp hands. "Let the pulse of energy traveling through our circle fill you with the spirit of the theater," she said. Then she squeezed Maureen's hand. Maureen squeezed the hand of the girl sitting next to her, who squeezed the next hand, and so on. "Close your eyes and draw in the energy of your fellow castmates," Ms. Hedley intoned, closing her own eyes and tipping her face to the ceiling. "*Be* the circle. *Be* the stage." Then she'd clapped her hands together twice. "Okay, cast, let's put on a show!"

I couldn't believe I had to do it all over again. "Is she serious?" I muttered, wondering if Ms. Hedley would notice if I hid under my seat.

"Every day, twice a day," Kayla said. "Welcome to the wonderful world of Alencia musical theater.

Starring everyone's favorite former hippie and her loyal disciple, Maureen Shepherd."

"So I guess she's been in the show before?" I asked.

"Oh, please. Maureen Shepherd *is* the show — at least according to Maureen Shepherd," Kayla said. She shook her head. "Who's going to compete with her, Lee 'n' Lee?" She pointed toward the two girls who'd run out to get Maureen a mug of hot tea.

"Sisters?" I asked.

She shook her head. "They wish. Emily and Natalie, aka Lee 'n' Lee, aka 'OMG we're totes going to be BFFs, like, forever!'" she simpered in a high, flighty voice. "They pretty much do whatever Maureen says, because they think she can get them better parts. Which she probably can, since she's got Ms. Hedley wrapped around her little finger. If Maureen doesn't like you —"

"If?" I laughed.

"Right. Since Maureen doesn't like you, you can pretty much count on Lee 'n' Lee acting like you're some kind of slime they accidentally stepped in."

While we waited for Ms. Hedley to call us into the circle, Kayla took me through the highs and lows (mostly lows, according to her) of the rest of the cast. That included Mark Castle, who never wore deodorant and was the very last person you wanted to get paired with during any kind of dance scene. Shayna Ryan, who always got cast as someone's mother. Maddie Crayne, whose dream was to act on a soap opera one day, even though she was so shy that she'd never even tried out for a speaking part.

"Giving New Girl the big, bad bullet points on *Monster Mash* madness?" a scrawny boy asked, popping up behind us. A girl with spiky brown hair and chunky purple hoop earrings sat down next to him.

"Did she get to the most important part yet?" she asked me. "Us?"

"Just saving the worst for last," Kayla said, winking.

The boy grinned. "Okay, but only one of us can be the worst, so who's it gonna be, me or her?" He propped his chin on his fist and gave us a mournful look. "Keep in mind, I never win anything, so you should probably take pity and pick me."

Kayla rolled her eyes. "Ruby Day, international superstar, meet Jaida and Sam. Or, as you may prefer to address them, Weird and Weirder."

"Hi," I said. It sounded so lame. But how was I supposed to know what to say? I hadn't made a new friend since third grade.

"Please, we're the only normal ones here," Sam said. "Stop lying to New Girl."

"Us?" Jaida asked, eyes wide. "Normal?"

Kayla shrugged. "Normal is overrated."

It was weird hearing Great-aunt Silva's favorite words coming out of this random girl's mouth. Good weird.

"So have you told her about our resident heart-throb yet?" Sam asked, nodding toward a short, skinny boy with shaggy black hair and a cocky grin. Lee 'n' Lee were fluttering around him. Sam nudged Jaida. "I'm told *some* girls think he's irresistible."

Jaida's cheeks turned bright pink. "I'm told *some* boys should stop talking before someone staples their mouth shut."

"That guy? A heartthrob?" I asked, surprised. He was kind of cute, but nothing special. I'd seen plenty of cuter guys around school — not that I was looking.

"My point exactly," Sam said, flexing a nonexistent muscle.

"As you may have noticed, not that many guys around here want to be in the school musical,"

Kayla said. I actually hadn't noticed, but now I realized there were only three or four guys in the whole cast. "And Anoop is definitely the best of them —"

"Hey!" Sam cut in, looking wounded.

"Sam, you're a worse singer than I am," Kayla said. "I didn't even think that was possible before I met you."

"It's true," he admitted. "I only tried out because Jaida made me."

He gave her a look that made me think he'd do pretty much anything Jaida asked him to — but Jaida didn't notice. She was still watching Anoop.

Kayla caught my eye, and shrugged. "Like I said, most of the girls are in love with him just because he can carry a tune."

"Most of the girls . . . but not you?"

Kayla stood up as Ms. Hedley beckoned us toward the Circle of Energy. "He's kind of a Conrad."

"As in Conrad Birdie, from *Bye Bye Birdie*?" I guessed.

"You got it," she said. "Kind of dim, extremely full of himself, and very much not my type."

"Let's join the Circle, dears," Ms. Hedley called.

I didn't want to have to get up — sitting there with Kayla and her friends, I could almost imagine that I was one of them. But they were just being nice to me because I was New Girl. Anything else was wishful thinking. The show, on the other hand, was real. Maybe I'd never been part of a group like that, but I was still part of a cast. That had always been enough.

"Your fellow cast members are your lifeline," Ms. Hedley said as we settled into the Circle of Energy. "Buoys of strength that will keep you afloat."

As everyone else closed their eyes, Kayla caught my eye and stuck out her tongue. I had to bite down on the inside of my cheeks to keep from bursting into laughter.

"The *thee-ate-or* is like life, my dears," Ms. Hedley droned. "No one can go it alone."

I still thought she was a flake. But — I glanced at Kayla again — maybe the flake had a point.

I managed to get through the next morning without any major disasters. Maybe it was the luck of the theater rubbing off on me, but for the first time I got my locker open on the third try, only got lost on the way to class once, and made it through a whole period of gym class softball without going up to bat. It was shaping up to be a better-than-awful day.

Then came French.

"Comprenez-vous?" Madame Johnson asked the class after spewing a long speech full of French mumbo jumbo. We all nodded, even though I was pretty sure none of us had *comprenez*-ed anything. Fortunately, she repeated herself in English. "Divide yourself into groups of two or three and write a short skit using the weather words learned today. I'll give you twenty minutes, and then we can perform."

The classroom started buzzing as people twisted around in their seats to choose their group. I stayed where I was, hoping that one of them would pick me.

No one did.

What is it about "choosing your own groups equals cruel and inhuman torture" that teachers don't understand?

"Oh, will you be working on your own, Ruby *cherie*?" Madame Johnson asked, once the rest of the class had paired off. "That should be no problem for *you*," she tittered. "I do hope the class isn't moving too slowly for you."

Madame Johnson had loved me from the

moment she found out I'd lived in Paris. She said my accent was perfect — of course, the only thing she'd ever heard me say was *Bonjour, je m'appelle* Ruby. (Hello, my name is Ruby.) After that, she did most of the talking.

"The class is great, Madame Johnson," I mumbled. "It's, uh, *très bien*."

She beamed. *"Oui, oui, très bien."* Then she said a bunch of other stuff I didn't understand. I just smiled and nodded until she walked away.

I slumped down in my chair and stared at my notebook, trying to figure out how I was supposed to perform a skit without a partner. A few desks away, I could hear Maureen bossing around her group. "No, just trust me, I know what I'm doing."

Bossy or not, I wished that she was in my group, because I definitely didn't know what I was doing. Anything would have been better than coming up with something on my own.

Wait a minute — *on my own.*

It was the title of my favorite song from *Les Miserables.* It also happened to be the song I'd memorized — in *French* — for that performance in the Louvre. Wasn't there a line in there about rain? That definitely counted as a weather word.

I started scribbling down all the words I could remember. This might actually work.

"C'est l'heure!" Madame Johnson announced. "Time's up! Now, who would like to go first?"

Maureen's hand shot into the air. The teacher gave her a thin smile. "Maureen, of course. And do I assume you have another Broadway extravaganza for us today?"

"*Bien sur*," Maureen said, towing the rest of her group toward the front of the room.

Bien sur. I was pretty sure that meant *of course*. My stomach clenched. If Maureen always did a Broadway thing, would Madame Johnson think I was copying her? Worse: Would *Maureen*?

Maureen started singing. She was on key and all, but her accent was *terrible*. (Even I know that's French for "terrible.") *"J'ai un cheval ici, il s'appelle Paul Revere,"* she sang. I didn't understand any of the words, but I recognized the melody. *Guys and Dolls* was one of my favorite shows.

Maureen finished her line and nudged one of her partners, a girl with dark blond hair who looked like she would rather crawl under a desk than sing in front of the whole class. But she opened her mouth and spit out a few creaky, off-key lines. *"Il y a un type qui a dit que s'il fait beau . . ."*

When the three of them finished, there was

a long pause, and then a few people clapped. Madame Johnson wasn't one of them. "Charming, as always." Her forehead crinkled. "And . . . what was that from? *The Phantom of the Opera*, perhaps? *The Sound of Music*?"

I couldn't tell whether Maureen was about to laugh or scream. "*Guys and Dolls*," she said. "You know, 'I got a horse right here, his name is Paul Revere'?"

"Right." Madame Johnson looked clueless. "Well, you got a few of your tenses wrong and we need to work on your pronunciation, but all in all, nice job."

Maureen took her seat, beaming. The other members of her group sat behind her and exchanged a glance that made me think next time they'd be working with someone else.

None of the other skits were much better. Maddie Crayne, from the *Monster Mash* cast, did a scene with Shayna Ryan and some other kids from the play, pretending they were all in the cast of a French soap opera. Maddie played a soap opera star who'd lost her voice — I guess so she didn't have to say any lines — with Shayna as her mother. (I couldn't wait to tell Kayla that she was right. Shayna really did always play someone's mom, even in French class.)

Anoop was in my class, too. Lucky me. *"Je suis . . . uh . . . uh . . . le hungry!"* he announced. He and some of the stairwell chocolate-milk boys were doing a lame skit about a rained-out barbecue. Only Anoop couldn't get any of his lines right. (Shocking, huh?) Whenever he forgot the French, he just threw in an English word. "Give-eh meee le hamburger, dude. Uh . . . *s'il vous plaît.*"

What's French for "one lame dude"?

"Who's next?" Madame Johnson asked, looking around the room. I tried to make myself invisible. "Ah, *magnifique.* Ruby!"

I sighed and walked slowly to the front of the room, hoping this wouldn't be a total disaster.

"This is a song called 'On My Own,'" I said. "But in French it's called *'Mon Histoire.'* My story." As I started singing, all the French lyrics I'd learned came back to me. *"Je suis toute seule encore une fois sans une ami,"* the song began.

I'm all alone again, without a friend.

The song was about a lonely girl who walked through the streets of Paris at night, imagining that her life was different. She loved the rain, because it turned the world into something beautiful. But every morning, she woke up to the truth: Her fantasies were just fantasies. The rain was just rain. And she was still on her own.

As I sang, I forgot everything around me. I tried to imagine that *I* was that girl, all by myself, dreaming of a better life.

It wasn't that hard to do.

When the applause started, I almost forgot where I was, and took a bow, like I was on a real stage. *"Magnifique!"* Madame Johnson cried, clapping loudly. Her head bobbed up and down as her bony arms flapped. *"Très bien! Très bien!"* she squawked. "Every word perfect! Maureen, perhaps next time you and Ruby can work together. She can give you some tips on your pronunciation."

Maureen glared at me. Like she didn't hate me enough already.

Maureen slipped out of the room as soon as the bell rang. I hurried to catch up with her. "I thought your *Guys and Dolls* thing was pretty cool," I told her.

"Yeah?" She scowled. "You were the only one. I guess we can't all be *magnifique*, huh?"

"You know, the only reason I got it all right was because I already had the lyrics memorized," I confessed. "I just used what I learned on tour."

Maureen rolled her eyes. "You don't have to brag about your tour every time you open your mouth. We all know you're a big star."

"I wasn't *bragging*! I was just trying to be nice. Obviously that was a big mistake."

For a second, Maureen almost looked sorry. But then Madame Johnson swooped down on us. "Ruby, *cherie*, come talk to me after school today, *s'il vous plaît*. I would love for you to perform your song as a representative of the French department at next week's Festival of Nations."

Maureen scowled. "*I'm* supposed to be the French department representative," she said. "Remember, I asked you about it in October? And you said it could be me."

Madame Johnson hesitated. "Ah . . . well, perhaps the two of you can work together. I'm sure Ruby could use some assistance. We'll discuss it later." She fluttered away before Maureen or I could say anything else.

"You can still do it if you want," I offered quietly. "I don't care. I don't even know what the Festival of Nations is."

"It's nothing," Maureen said. "Just another chance for you to show everyone how *talented* you are. You'll love it."

"You don't know that," I snapped. "You don't know anything about me."

"I know you think you're better than me,"

Maureen said. "You think you're destined to be some big star, and that I'm just a big nobody."

I didn't say anything.

"But at this school, *I'm* the star," she said.

I couldn't help myself. "For *now*."

Maureen's cheeks turned red. She took a couple deep breaths, and when she spoke, her voice was calm. Maybe she was a better actor than I'd thought. "See you at rehearsal," she said. "Hope you're enjoying the *chorus*."

It turned out the Festival of Nations was the school's "celebration of world culture." That didn't actually explain anything, but I didn't ask any questions. As far as I was concerned, the faster I could get out of Madame Johnson's classroom, the better. I just told her I'd do it, whatever it was — even if it meant doing a duet with Maureen. Then I ran off to rehearsal.

Maureen glared at me when I slipped in a few minutes late, then gave me the silent treatment for the rest of the afternoon.

When we finished the second Circle of Energy, Ms. Hedley stopped us before we could leave. "Before you go anywhere, my artistic geniuses, a representative from the PTA is here to make a few announcements." She ushered in a round, red-haired woman. "Mrs. Shepherd, the stage is yours."

"Shepherd?" I whispered to Kayla. "As in *Maureen* Shepherd?"

Kayla nodded. "Like daughter, like mother."

"What do you mean?" I asked.

"You'll see."

Mrs. Shepherd explained how the PTA was going to help out with ticket sales and selling ads in the *Monster Mash* program. "As you know, the PTA traditionally also pays for the cast costumes. Unfortunately, due to some fund-raising setbacks, we'll only be able to supply costumes for the principals this year."

"Dude, why does the principal need a costume?" Anoop shouted. Lee 'n' Lee, who were sitting on either side of him, giggled. He slapped hands with both of them.

"A *principal* role is a leading role," Mrs. Shepherd said. "So, for example, the star of your production — the very talented Maureen Shepherd — has a *principal* role. Stand up, Maureen. Show them what a principal looks like."

Maureen blushed furiously and stayed seated, staring down at the stage.

Kayla and I locked eyes. "What's the opposite of Mini Me?" Kayla whispered.

I shrugged. "Maxi Me?"

"That's what she is — a Maxi Maureen!"

I burst into giggles, shushing her.

"If you're in the chorus, I'm afraid you'll have to make your own costumes," Mrs. Shepherd continued, when it became obvious Maureen wasn't going to stand up.

"Glad I'm not in the chorus," Anoop called out. "This dude doesn't sew."

The Lees giggled louder this time.

"Don't worry about making your costume perfect," Mrs. Shepherd said. "After all, the audience will be paying attention to the principals." She said it sweetly, but it still hurt. Because I knew she was right. When the curtain rose, no one would be looking at me, they'd be looking at Maureen. *The star.*

When Mrs. Shepherd was finished, she pulled a big stack of envelopes out of her purse. "Why don't I hand these out for you, dear," she suggested to Maureen.

"Mo-oooom." When Maureen said it, the word sounded like it had about six syllables. "I'll meet you in the car, okay?"

"Okay, but don't be long, we're late for your dance lesson."

Once her mother was gone, Maureen started handing out envelopes to a bunch of the kids in the cast. Not all of them — just the ones with important roles.

"It's next weekend," she whispered loudly to one of the Lees. "But keep it to yourself, because I couldn't invite everyone. You know how it is." She glanced at me and Kayla. "Some things are just for the *principals*."

"What do you think it is?" I asked Kayla.

She shrugged. "Do you care?"

"Of course not," I said. At least, I didn't *want* to care that Maureen wasn't inviting me to her dumb whatever-it-was. Or that I was going to have to make my own costume. Or that I was just in the chorus, with people like Kayla, who might have been awesome, but still couldn't sing a note. I didn't want to care about any of it.

But I couldn't help myself: I did.

Chapter 5

"Come on, Mom, you're not really going to make me go to this thing, right?" Alana whined. We were already in the car, halfway there, so there wasn't much chance that Mom was kidding around.

Still, just in case: "If she doesn't have to go, I shouldn't have to go either," I pointed out.

"Enough!" Mom snapped.

Alana and I exchanged a glance. Mom got kind of cranky when she drove. (But she got even crankier when Dad drove, which is why he was sitting in the passenger seat.)

"Ruby, you're going to the Festival of Nations because you told your teacher you would. And Alana, you're going to support your sister."

"Yeah, because I've never seen her sing before," Alana muttered. "When's the last time she came to one of my soccer games? Oh, right. Never."

I glared at her. "Maybe if you didn't act like such a —"

"Girls!" my mother said loudly. "Can we just have a peaceful, pleasant ride? Just for a few minutes, pretend you like each other."

"Think about what a wonderful educational opportunity this will be," my father said in a voice that made it very clear that he wished he were home watching TV. "And how much joy we all take in celebrating the cultures of our world."

"Don't encourage them," Mom said — but in the rearview mirror, I caught a glimpse of a smile.

As soon as we got to school, Alana ran off to join some friends. Great, I thought, walking into the building sandwiched between my parents. She doesn't even go to this school and she still has more friends here than I do.

"You could give Alana a break, you know," my mother said quietly.

"Me?" I asked. "Give *her* a break?"

"She missed you while you were gone," my mom said. "It's been hard for her."

It's been hard for me, too, I thought. But it was best not to argue when Mom was in wisdom-dispensing mode.

"And she's changed a lot," she added.

I snorted a laugh. "Tell me about it."

"You've changed, too," my dad pointed out mildly. "Maybe it's just going to take the two of you some time to get back to where you were."

"Are you giving her this little speech, too?" I asked.

My mom paused. "You're older," she said. "And hopefully a little more mature."

Right. But in this case, I wasn't the one with the problem. Whatever was going on in Alana's weird head, talking to me wasn't going to fix it.

Maybe if I hadn't spent the last two years traveling all over the world, the Festival of Nations wouldn't have seemed so lame.

But I doubt it.

The cafeteria tables had been shoved out of the way to make space for a bunch of booths, each with its own flag draped over the side. The kids at the Italy booth were handing out mini pizza bagels. The ones at the Greece booth were dressed in homemade togas, reciting scenes from the *Odyssey*. My parents and I stopped short at the Mexico booth, gaping at the kids in sombreros, offering us microwave tortilla bites.

"This is supposed to represent the culture of Mexico?" my dad asked, sounding half amused and half horrified.

My mom rolled her eyes. "Apparently, we missed this part last time we visited."

I'd been to Mexico twice, once with my mom to meet some cousins she hadn't seen since she was little, and once with my whole family to go to a wedding.

Neither trip involved microwave tortilla bites.

"Does this mean we can go home now?" I asked hopefully.

My mom gave me her patented *nice try* look. "If you don't approve, maybe you should volunteer to help organize next year's festival."

"Um, yeah. Maybe." Not going to happen. By next year, I'd be long gone. Back onstage, back on tour. Back to the *real* world, where Italian pizza didn't involve bagels.

I left my parents sipping some hot chocolate by "Switzerland" and wandered off to find Madame Johnson. I wanted to show her the subtitle cards I'd made and make sure they were all right. (They were kind of like cue cards, only instead of showing my lines, they had the song's English lyrics on them. That way, the audience would know what Maureen and I were singing.)

"Aren't you going to say hello to your favorite kiwi bird?" Jaida called out as I passed by the New Zealand booth.

"Go ahead, squawk hello to Not-So-New Girl," Sam teased.

The girl standing between them — the one with brown feathers taped all over her body and a giant cardboard beak strapped to her face — gave a halfhearted squawk.

"Kayla?" I burst into giggles. "What are you *doing*?"

"It's for extra credit, okay?" she growled, glaring at Jaida and Sam. "Look, it could have been worse — I could be a kangaroo."

"So beak beats pouch?" I asked, laughing even harder when I spotted her webbed feet. "You sure about that?"

"I don't know, I think she looks quite . . . feathery," Sam teased, ruffling her feathers.

"Also beaky," Jaida added.

Before I could come up with another silly bird adjective, Anoop strolled past. He was flanked by the Lees, who were giggling at everything he said.

"Perfect," Kayla muttered.

"Dude, check out the birdbrain!" Anoop shouted. Natalie and Emily cackled.

I glared after them. It was one thing for *us* to tease Kayla, but —

Wait, I thought suddenly, I'm part of an *us*?

I liked the sound of that.

"Aw, don't be shy, little birdie," Anoop cooed as Kayla tried to duck behind those of us who weren't in embarrassing costumes. "Are you going to fly away?"

Kayla groaned and straightened up. She glared at Anoop. "Kiwi birds can't fly, you dope. Try again."

Anoop looked surprised.

"Come on," she challenged him. "I'm sure you can come up with something better than that."

"Uh . . ." Natalie and Emily gazed at Anoop, waiting for him to come up with something good. "Dude, you're dressed like a bird," he said finally.

The Lees laughed. But this time, I was pretty sure they were laughing at Anoop.

When I finally found the France booth, Alana was there, too, stuffing her face with croissants and chatting up Madame Johnson.

"Ah, and here she is now!" Madame Johnson twittered as I arrived. "*Bonjour, cherie*. I was just telling your sister what a wonderful performance you and Maureen will be putting on for us tonight."

I tried to smile. I was pretty sure Maureen was just as excited about this duet as I was. Not at all.

"You must be so proud of your big sister," Madame Johnson said, turning back to Alana.

Alana grunted something.

"Did you bring the subtitle cards?" Madame Johnson asked.

I nodded and pulled out the stack of poster board. "They got a little wrinkled." I apologized, unfolding them and trying to smooth out the creases. "Maybe I shouldn't have shoved them into my backpack. . . ."

Pas de problème," Madame Johnson said. I figured that either meant "Horrible problem," or "No problem." She didn't look too mad, so hopefully it was the second one. She stretched out the subtitle cards and placed a stack of books on top of them. "We'll just flatten them out a bit, and by showtime, I'm sure they'll be fine." She turned to Alana. "Are you a good singer, too?"

"About as good as Ruby is at French," Alana said.

"Ah, then you must be *magnifique!"* She beamed.

Alana shot me a wicked grin. "That's not exactly what I —"

"Okay!" I said loudly, clapping my hands around her shoulders. "I should probably find Maureen and start warming up. Alana, why don't you come with me?" *Before Madame Johnson figures out that I speak about as much French as a French poodle.*

"Maybe I was wrong about this whole festival thing," Alana said in an annoyingly chipper voice as I steered her away from the booth. "It's turning out to be much more fun than I thought."

Maureen and I stood backstage, waiting for the kids from the Italian department to finish their skit. Everyone had filed out of the cafeteria and into the auditorium for the performances. I peeked out from behind the curtain. It looked like half the school was out there.

Not that I was nervous or anything. I'd sung this song in front of the entire French parliament. Singing it for a bunch of middle schoolers and their parents didn't seem like a big deal. Maureen, on the other hand, looked a little green.

"You sure you don't want to bring a copy of the lyrics onstage?" I whispered. "Just in case?"

"I *told* you I had them memorized," she hissed.

"I'll be fine. You just worry about holding up the subtitle cards in the right order."

The cards! I'd left them back in the cafeteria.

"What?" Maureen snapped. "You don't have the cards? Madame Johnson's going to kill us!"

"I have them," I said defensively. "I mean, I don't have them *with* me, but they're in the cafeteria, at the French booth. I'll just go get them —"

"No, *I'll* go," Maureen said. "You'll probably get distracted on the way there and forget where you're going. I told Madame Johnson not to make this a duet." She shook her head. "I thought you were supposed to be some kind of professional."

"It's not a big deal —"

Maureen scowled. "Maybe not to you." She ran off to find the cards.

Minutes passed.

The Italian skit ended.

"You're up!" someone whispered, giving me a little push toward the stage.

Where was Maureen?

Great, I thought miserably. Now she's going to miss the whole thing and have another reason to hate me.

I slipped through the curtain — just as Maureen showed up, panting. She shoved the stack of poster board into my hand. "You're welcome."

Then we were onstage together, side by side, smiling like we didn't hate each other. Madame Johnson gave us a thumbs-up from the front row.

I held the wrinkled posters over my head, and we began to sing. "*Je suis toute seule* —" I broke off as the audience burst into laughter. I glanced at Maureen. She looked as clueless as I was.

We started singing again, but when I got to the next line — and the next subtitle card — the audience roared even louder.

Suddenly, I had a horrifying thought.

Without pausing in the song, I lowered the posters. The one I'd been displaying was supposed to read, *Without a friend, without anything to do*. I knew, because I'd written it myself.

But this card read:

I'm a geek.

Still singing and beaming out at the tittering audience, I flipped through the rest of the cards.

I pick my nose.

I stink. Literally.

The thick red block letters disguised the handwriting. But I didn't need handwriting to know who'd done it. I looked over at Maureen again, who hadn't missed a beat.

She glared back, like this was all my fault.

But it was so obviously hers.

As we made it through the rest of the song, the audience gradually stopped laughing. I never stopped fuming.

We finished the song and took a bow. "I guess you thought that was funny," Maureen muttered over the applause.

"Hilarious," I said through gritted teeth. No way was I going to give her the satisfaction of acting totally humiliated.

"I just can't believe you're this desperate for attention," she hissed.

"Me?"

"You made us both look like idiots!"

"Maybe you should have thought of that before you sabotaged me," I pointed out.

"You think I did that?" she asked. "You're seriously insane."

"Magnifique!" Madame Johnson said, climbing up onto the stage with us. "Weren't they wonderful?" she cried to the audience. "Go on, girls, take another bow."

We joined hands, smiled, and soaked in the applause. That's what you do when you're a pro. As long as you're onstage, you act like you're the best friend your costar ever had.

You wait until you're offstage to get her back.

☆ *Chapter 6* ☆

The good news is that by the next day, no one was talking about our performance at the Festival of Humiliation.

The bad news is that by the next day, no one was talking about our performance at the Festival of Humiliation.

It's not that I wanted people to be snickering and pointing as I walked down the hall, but you know what they say: There's no such thing as bad publicity. When you're a star, you have to get used to people talking about you. And I guess when you're a nobody, you have to get used to people *not* talking about you.

Being a nobody wasn't something I planned to get used to.

Even though the rest of the week passed without any disasters, I was happier than ever to hit the weekend. Two blissful days away from lockers, cafeteria food, pop quizzes — and, most blissfully, from Maureen Shepherd.

Most mornings, everyone in my family woke up at different times. Breakfast meant grabbing some food on the way out the door. But on Saturdays, we all ate together.

I lifted my plate of eggs and held it out to my father. "I asked for these poached, but they're kind of scrambled," I said. "Could you . . . ?"

He shot me a steely glare. "Yes?"

"Dad, I *love* your eggs," Alana simpered, narrowing her eyes at me. "They're delicious."

"Thanks," my dad said. "But we're waiting to hear what fault your sister finds with the cooking."

"Um, nothing." I set down the plate. "Thanks for making breakfast."

My dad smiled and patted me on the head, even though he knew I hated that. "You're welcome."

I'd been home for three weeks, but it was still hard to remember not to treat my parents' cooking like room service, which meant sending it back when it wasn't exactly what I wanted. And, since my parents were such bad cooks, it was almost *never* what I wanted.

The phone rang, just as my mother was sitting down to eat.

"Hello?" she said into the receiver. Then she laughed. "No, there is no Mrs. Day — it's Davenstein, actually. Melina Davenstein. Ruby just . . . well, it's a long story."

So the call was about me. I thought back over the school week. Had I done something to get in trouble?

My mom's eyes widened. "Really?" she asked, sounding surprised. "Well, how lovely of you." She scribbled something down on a piece of paper. "Got it. I know exactly where that is."

She hung up the phone, and gave me that proud-mother look.

"Well?" I said, trying to keep my voice steady. Could it be someone calling about an audition? "Who was it?"

My mom sat down at the table and turned toward my dad, smiling. "It seems your daughter has made a friend."

He grinned. "If you're talking about *your* daughter, you must be mistaken. She hates everyone and everything at that school of hers. Doesn't she tell us so every day?"

"Apparently we've been underestimating the power of her sunny personality," my mom teased.

"Can someone just tell me who called?" I asked, not feeling particularly sunny.

"Tell the truth, Mom," Alana said. "You hired someone to be friends with her, right?"

I couldn't take it anymore. If it was Kayla, why didn't she want to talk to me herself? And if it wasn't Kayla . . . well, there weren't really any other options, were there? *Mom —*"

"As I was saying," my mother interrupted. "That was a Mrs. Shepherd, wanting to know if you'd come to her daughter's sleepover party tonight. She says your friend Maureen would be delighted if you came."

I almost spit out my eggs. "Are you sure she wasn't looking for some other Ruby Day? Because Maureen Shepherd does *not* want me at her party. I guarantee you."

"Not according to her mother. She says Maureen is really excited to get the chance to hear more about your experiences on tour. It sounds like she really admires you. Isn't that sweet?"

Now my sister was the one who almost spit out her breakfast. "Yeah, Ruby, isn't that sweet?" she asked. "You have your own personal groupie."

I ignored her. "Mom, Maureen *hates* me."

My dad opened his mouth in a perfect circle of fake horror. "How could anyone hate *you*, my perfect little darling?"

"Ask her," I said sourly. "If she didn't hate me, why would she sabotage me at the Festival of Nations?"

Alana's fork clattered against her plate. "You think that was *her*?"

"Who else could it be?" I pointed out. "She's out to get me."

Alana rolled her eyes. "It's not like it was a big deal or anything."

"Oh, really? She only humiliated me in front of the whole school," I snapped.

"I'm just saying, I'm sure she wasn't trying to ruin your life."

"Why are you defending Maureen, anyway?" I asked. "You don't even know her."

Instead of answering, Alana shoved a giant forkful of omelet into her mouth, chewing *verrrrrry slooooowly*, until I got the message. She was done.

"Do you have proof that this girl is the one who did it?" my mom asked, looking concerned.

"Because if so, I should really talk to her mother —"

"No!" I yelped. Seriously, how do parents end up so totally clueless? "Look, I don't have any evidence," I admitted. "I just know it was her."

My mom didn't seem convinced. "You could be wrong about her. If she hated you, why would she invite you to her party?"

"Mom." I breathed a loud, heavy sigh. "I don't know what's going on, but I am *not* invited to that party."

"Well, that should make things pretty awkward when you show up," my mom said.

"What?"

"I told her you were going, and you are," she said.

"Am *not*."

"Very mature," Alana jeered. "You got so grown up while you were away."

"Leave me alone!" I snapped.

"Rebecca!" My mother didn't look proud anymore. "Your sister was just joking. There's no need to be rude to her."

"Rude to *her*?" I couldn't believe it. "Are you even listening? Don't you —"

"Becca," my dad said quietly but firmly. "Just let it go."

I slouched down in my chair.

"You need friends," my mom said. "You've been back for three weeks now, and you haven't gone anywhere but school."

"I went to the mall last weekend," I argued.

"Yeah, with *Mom*," Alana pointed out. "Like that counts."

"Thank you, dear," Mom told her. "I'll keep that in mind the next time you beg me to take you on a shopping spree."

"Why can't you all just leave me alone?" I said. "Let me do what I want and —"

"What?" my mother shot back. "And run away, halfway around the world where there's no one to tell you what to do?"

"Sounds like a good idea to me," Alana said.

I crossed my arms. "Me too."

"Well, too bad," my mom said. Her face was pale and she kept running her hands through her hair, like she always did when her temper was about to flare. "You're here now. And I'm not your director, I'm not your backstage crew, I'm not your maid — I'm your *mother*. If that means you have to do chores and eat scrambled eggs and go to school and do some things you don't want to do, well, that's just too bad. Your father and I are just trying to do what's best for you. If you can't see that, maybe you can just *trust* us a little."

Whoa. My mom never yelled — at least not at me. Neither of my parents had yelled at me for years. Whenever I came home for a visit, they treated me like just that: a visitor.

Is it weird that I sort of missed the yelling?

I sighed. "I do trust you. I just think you don't know what's going on here. Maureen does *not* want me at that party."

"I'm getting the sense you don't like Maureen that much," my father said mildly.

"Understatement of the year," I muttered.

The corners of his lips twitched, like he was trying not to smile. "And you're pretty sure she doesn't want you at her party?"

"*Very* sure."

"In fact, having you there might even *ruin* her party?" my father suggested.

"Probably."

"Huh." My dad turned back to his breakfast, scooping up a big forkful of eggs. "Interesting."

Suddenly, it hit me. It was just so . . . devious and un-Dad-like.

"Are you saying that I should go to that party *because* Maureen doesn't want me there? Just to ruin her night?"

My father opened his eyes extra wide. "I would never suggest such a thing," he said innocently. "I was just asking some questions."

"Huh," I said, echoing him. "Interesting."

My mom looked from my dad to me and back again, wavering between disgust and amusement. "So we're agreed? You'll go?"

I sighed. I had to admit, my mom was right — I didn't have any friends. Sure, there was Kayla . . . but I couldn't stop thinking about something she'd said on Friday about Jaida and Sam: "They're cool, but they're just show friends, you know? We hang out during rehearsals, but once the show's over, they usually do their own thing."

Is that what Kayla and I were, too? Show friends?

That was pretty much all I'd had for the last four years. And it had never bothered me much before. Why should it bother me now?

It just did.

Not that I was planning to make friends with Maureen or anyone else she'd invited to her party. But I'd been trying to figure out the perfect way to get back at Maureen. Maybe this was my golden opportunity.

I had to admit, anything would be better than

another TV night on the couch next to my parents.

"Fine," I said, still a little bitter. "I'll go. But don't expect me to have any fun."

My mom grinned. "The thought never crossed my mind."

"Should I come in with you?" my mom asked as we pulled up in front of Maureen's house.

"Um, no thanks." I didn't know much about the whole friend thing, and this was the first noncast party I'd been to since I was nine years old, but I wasn't completely clueless. There was no way I was risking total embarrassment by showing up with my *mother*.

Maureen's house was about the same size as mine, but hers was a lot older. My house may have been ten years old, but it still felt brand-new, fresh off the assembly line, complete with new-house smell. It had no personality — no creaky stairs, no paint hidden behind the wallpaper. Great-aunt Silva would say it had no story. Maureen's house, on the other hand, looked like it had a million stories. The weathered brick walls were bounded by tall, leafy trees that scraped the sloping roof. A scuffed footpath of multicolored stones wove through overgrown grass, stretching from the driveway to the front door. The welcome mat read COME TO THIS HOUSE, BE ONE OF US. I grinned, recognizing the lyrics from *Tommy*. Maybe this wasn't such alien territory after all.

I set down my sleeping bag and rang the bell.

The door flew open, and Mrs. Shepherd flung her arms around me. "Ruby!" she trilled. "Come in, come in." She turned toward the stairs and shouted for Maureen. "Come on down, your friend is here!"

I wondered where everyone else was. Upstairs, maybe? Probably brainstorming ways to torture me while I slept.

Good luck, I thought. I had spent all afternoon doing research on sleepover pranks, and my duffel bag was packed with countermeasures: lime Jell-O, digital camera, mini-flashlight, red permanent marker, and a can of shaving cream. They couldn't get me if I got them first.

Maureen trudged down the stairs. "Hey," she muttered, not looking at me.

"It's so wonderful to have you here," Mrs. Shepherd said eagerly. She led me into the living room and patted the arm of a blue, overstuffed chair. "Sit down, sit down. Maureen's been telling me all about you and your fabulous career."

"She has?" I asked, surprised.

Maureen's face flushed to match her hair.

"It's a real honor for her to sing alongside you in the school musical," Mrs. Shepherd said. "Of course, you must be headed back on tour soon."

Now it was my turn to blush and look away.

"Mom, come on," Maureen whined. "She doesn't want to talk about that stuff. Let us go upstairs."

Mrs. Shepherd chuckled. "You're right, of course. You kids go have fun." She leaned toward me and lowered her voice to a stage whisper. "But maybe later you can sneak down here for a little chitchat. Maureen and I can always use advice from a real live expert, right, Maureen?"

Maureen rolled her eyes. "Right." She jerked her head toward the stairs, then headed up without waiting to see if I would follow her. By the time I caught up, I could see she was furious.

Uh-oh, I thought. How mad was she that I had crashed her party? And what did she have planned for revenge?

"She is *so* embarrassing," Maureen fumed as soon as we were upstairs. She pulled me into her room, then slammed the door shut behind us. "Sorry."

"Sorry for what?"

Her eyes widened. "My mom." Maureen sighed. "Sometimes I think it's her mission in life to humiliate me."

Like you humiliated me? I thought. But I was stuck at her house for the night, at her mercy. I kept my mouth shut.

"She wasn't so bad," I assured her instead.

Maureen shook her head. "That was nothing. Wait until she shows up with the *Bye Bye Birdie*–themed snacks."

I swallowed a laugh. "You're joking."

Maureen's mouth lifted in an almost-smile. "I wish. She'll leave us alone until she can't stand it anymore, which will probably be" — she glanced at the clock — "about ten minutes."

We both giggled, and I suddenly felt a tiny bit less weird.

"Uh . . . where's everyone else?" I asked hesitantly. Maybe they were hiding. I could picture Lee 'n' Lee huddled in the closet, waiting to leap out at me like two lions attacking their prey.

Maureen plopped onto her bed. "I'm guessing they're drinking strawberry smoothies by Allie Ferguson's pool."

"What?"

"You know — Allie Ferguson's party?"

I looked blank.

"You *do* know who Allie Ferguson is, right?"

"Not really," I admitted. "I think she's in my math class. Does she have brown hair?"

Maureen looked at me in disbelief, like I'd admitted I didn't know who Ethel Merman was. (For the record: Ethel Merman, born 1908, died 1984, star of *Gypsy*, *Annie Get Your Gun*, *Anything Goes*, and pretty much everything else. Considered one of the greatest divas in Broadway history. Great-aunt Silva's personal hero.)

"She's *blond*," Maureen said bitterly. "And popular, and lives in this giant mansion on the north side of town, and every few months she throws a giant party. Everyone who's anyone gets invited."

"Oh." I looked down. So it was official: I was a nobody.

"I wasn't invited either." Maureen balled her hands into fists. "I told my mom no one would come to this stupid sleepover. She thinks that just because I'm the star of the musical, people automatically like —" She stopped abruptly. "Never mind."

We stared at each other in silence for a moment. I wondered if she felt as awkward as I did.

"So, um, your room is pretty cool," I said finally. And even though I was just trying to come up with a way to break the silence, it was true. My bedroom was almost empty, like a hotel room. Maureen's room was more like a living, breathing extension of Maureen. Every inch of wall space was covered.

I wandered over to the wall by her bed, which was papered with photos of Maureen onstage. I could tell from the costumes which parts she was playing — Maria in *The Sound of Music*, Eliza Doolittle in *My Fair Lady*, Elphaba in *Wicked*. All different costumes, different shows, different ages. But in every show, Maureen was obviously the star. "You've been in a lot of stuff."

Maureen shrugged. "School, summer camp, community theater, you know. My mom thinks the more parts I play, the better."

"Wish my mom felt that way," I murmured.

"Trust me, you don't. She made me put those up there, you know. If I had my way, the whole room would look like that." She waved her arm at the opposite wall, which was covered floor to ceiling in Broadway playbills.

When I got closer, my eyes bugged out. They were all *signed*. "You've been to this many shows?"

Maureen shook her head. "I write away for them," she said, sounding a little embarrassed. "I kind of collect them. That probably sounds weird."

"It sounds awesome." I noticed a playbill for *Les Miserables* taped up just above my head, and pointed at it. "You know, I was —" I stopped, reminding myself that every time I said something about my career, Maureen thought I was bragging.

"You were in the LA production of *Les Miz*," she said. "I know. So . . ." She paused. This is it, I thought. She's finally going to admit what she did.

"I guess that was probably more exciting than our performance at the Festival of Nations," she said with a half smile.

Why bring it up if she wasn't going to apologize? "Less exciting, and less humiliating," I said pointedly.

"So you really didn't make those posters yourself?" she asked.

"Of course I didn't! *You* did."

"Why do you keep saying that? Why would I sabotage my own performance?"

"I don't know — maybe you're just really bad at evil plans," I snapped.

95

"Maybe you're really bad at playing amateur detective," she shot back.

"You're the only one who could have done it," I insisted. "And the only one who *would* have."

Maureen stalked over to her door, like she was about to open it and toss me out of her room. "If you think I'm so crazy, why did you even come tonight?"

"Because my mom made me!" I flung the words at her without thinking.

She looked like I'd slapped her. Then her face went blank. "Oh, yeah? Well, *my* mom made me invite you," she said coldly.

Like I hadn't already figured that out. Still, I was surprised to discover that it hurt. "Why?"

Maureen sagged against the wall. "She thinks you can help turn me into some big-time star. It's the only reason she ever does anything."

"I don't know what you're complaining about," I said. "Do you know how awesome it is to have a mom that actually *supports* your career? My mom doesn't get it at all. She just wants me to be *normal*."

Maureen sighed. "Please. I *wish* that was all my mom wanted. But it's like she never got to be some big Broadway star, so now it's her mission in life to make me into one." She rolled her eyes. "News flash, Mom. It's my life, not yours."

"I'm sure she's not that bad," I said.

She glared at me. "What do you know?"

I glared back. "I know you don't know how good you've got it."

The door swung open. "It's your director!" Maureen's mother tittered, poking her head into the room. "Treats!" she announced proudly, holding out a plate of cookies and cakes. "We've got Conrad Birdie Bundt cake, 'Honestly Sincere' soufflé, and 'What's the Matter with Kids Today?' cookies." She winked at me. "I know that was your big musical number."

Maureen caught my eye, raised her eyebrows, and we both burst into laughter.

I had to admit it, Mrs. Shepherd actually *was* that bad. Maybe worse.

"What?" she asked, totally confused.

"Nothing," Maureen and I chorused, laughing even harder.

When her mother left us to munch on the ridiculous but tasty *Bye Bye Birdie*–themed treats, I sank down on Maureen's bed. "Okay, you win," I said. "Your mom's kind of . . ."

"A total freak?" Maureen offered helpfully.

I grinned and popped a cookie into my mouth. "Ooo mfaf foo mpfit —"

"Swallow," Maureen suggested.

I did. "I said, you have to admit that she's a pretty good baker."

We started laughing again, and it hit me like a ton of bricks (and I mean the real kind, not the Styrofoam ones from the props department): I was actually having fun.

"So, what do you want to do now?" Maureen asked, once we'd gobbled up all the treats.

"I don't know," I admitted. "I haven't been to too many sleepover parties." Or *any*.

Maureen shrugged. "I guess we could do makeovers, or watch some music videos, or talk about guys or something."

"Well . . . I guess we could, if you wanted." It sounded like torture.

Maureen laughed. "Not unless you want to talk about what a sweaty-handed, tone-deaf egomaniac Anoop Shah is."

"But doesn't everyone think he's *sooooo* cute?" I pointed out.

Maureen grinned. "You want to know who has the school's biggest crush on Anoop?"

I leaned forward, sure I was about to score some excellent gossip. "Who?"

"Anoop. Once I caught him talking to the mirror, telling himself how great he was."

"No way."

Maureen held up her hand like she was taking a solemn pledge. "I swear on my *Wicked* soundtrack that I'm telling the truth."

"You like *Wicked*?" I asked, remembering how much Kayla hated it. I'd thought maybe I was lame for liking it.

"Who doesn't?" Maureen started scrolling through the playlist on her computer. "It's almost as good as *Rent* and *Miss Saigon*."

"Oh, it's totally better than *Rent*."

"No way." She shook her head firmly. "Not possible."

"See, now I can't trust your taste," I teased.

"My taste is impeccable. Try me."

"*The Phantom of the Opera*?" I said.

"Overrated."

"*Oklahoma.*"

"Thumbs-up."

"Steven Sondheim," I challenged her.

"Early or late?" she shot back.

"Post-*Gypsy*, pre-*Company*," I said.

She gave him two thumbs-up. "But thumbs-down for the later stuff. I don't think anyone actually likes it. They just think pretending to like it makes them sound smart." She narrowed her eyes. "Okay, my turn. *Avenue Q*."

"Awesome," I said.

"*The Sound of Music*."

I stuck my finger down my throat.

She wrinkled her nose. "Are you kidding?"

"*The hills are alive with . . . the sound of me puking*," I sang in a high falsetto.

She crossed her arms. "Fine. Agree to disagree. How about *Singin' in the Rain*?"

I sighed. "Oh, I love that. I haven't seen it in forever."

"I have it on DVD," Maureen said. "We could watch it, if you want."

"I want," I said, nodding eagerly. "Definitely."

We dragged our sleeping bags in front of the giant TV in her den. The picture quality was so good, it seemed like Gene Kelly was right there in the room with us, singing and dancing in the rain.

"We should totally do this show next year," Maureen said suddenly, about an hour into the movie. "I bet I could convince Ms. Hedley."

"Not possible," I said.

"I know she seems like a total flake, but she's actually really into the whole school musical thing," Maureen said. "And she promised to help me become a star. So if I convince her that *Singin' in the Rain* is the way to do it —"

"I didn't mean that," I explained. "I meant that *Singin' in the Rain* is about a guy who can dance — can you picture Anoop in the lead?"

"Oh. Good point." Maureen giggled. "He'd probably fall off the stage. Plus, can you imagine all those tone-deaf chorus klutzes trying to learn the steps? Total disaster."

She must have seen my expression in the glow of the television. "I'm not talking about *you*, obviously."

But I wasn't thinking about me. I was thinking about Kayla. Jaida and Sam, too. Suddenly, I felt kind of weird, laughing about the show with Maureen. Almost like I was being disloyal. Especially since staying up all night watching old movie musicals was exactly the kind of thing Kayla would have loved. "The chorus is better than you give them credit for," I said.

"Look, it's nothing personal," Maureen said. "Some people are just more talented than others."

"And some people are just more obnoxious than others."

There was a pause, like Maureen was trying to decide whether I'd just declared war. I steeled myself.

But instead of attacking, she laughed. "You may be right. What can I say? It's a gift." But when she spoke again, she didn't sound like she was joking. She sounded worried. "Am I really *that* obnoxious?"

"Truth?"

"Truth."

"Well . . ." I grinned. "Define *that*."

"I swear I didn't sabotage those posters," Maureen said suddenly. "I would never do that to someone. And you *know* I'd never do it to myself."

"You know what's weird?" I asked. "I believe you."

We were silent for a minute, watching Gene Kelly dance across the screen with some seriously un-Anoop-like grace. "Hey, can I ask you something?" I said quietly.

"I guess."

"Why do you even want to do the musical? With your mom and all — if you hate it so much, why not just quit?"

Maureen sat up abruptly, almost getting trapped by her oversize sleeping bag. "Who said I hated it?"

"Um, you."

"No, I hate the way my mom's totally obsessed. I hate how she's always dragging me to auditions and dance lessons and singing lessons and a million other things. I don't hate being onstage. That's different. That's . . . well, you know."

"Yeah." And I did.

The thing that happened onstage, when the curtain opened and the lights came up? It wasn't anything you could put into words. You either got it or you didn't.

Maureen did.

When we finished *Singin' in the Rain*, we popped in *Showboat*, then *Fiddler on the Roof*, then *West Side Story*. Around three A.M., we finally drifted off to sleep during the overture of *Oklahoma*. The next thing I knew, it was morning.

Everything felt different with the sun up. In the dark, with the TV blaring our favorite songs, Maureen and I had something in common. But in the daylight, it was too easy to remember that we weren't actually friends. That she hadn't even invited me to her "party" in the first place.

We didn't talk much at breakfast. Then again,

her mom talked enough for all of us. As Maureen slunk lower and lower in her seat, her mom raved about almost every role Maureen had ever played. "We've been to a lot of professional auditions, but no luck yet," she said finally. "I'm sure it's only a matter of time, though. She's so talented." She beamed at her daughter.

"Mom, please stop." Maureen looked miserable.

"Don't be embarrassed, honey," her mom said. "I'm sure it took Ruby a few auditions before she got her big break."

I tried to catch Maureen's eye, but she refused to look up from her plate of pancakes.

"Sure," she mumbled. "I'm sure it's just a matter of time before *we're* rich and famous."

Fortunately, I spotted my mom's car pulling up outside. I jumped out of my seat.

Maureen walked me to the door.

"So, I'll, uh, see you at school tomorrow, I guess?" I said.

"Yeah. See you." She hesitated. "Sorry again about my mom, and the whole 'party' thing."

"I had fun," I assured her. "I mean it."

"Really?" She looked surprised.

I raised my hand like I was taking a pledge. "I swear on your amazing collection of musical DVDs."

"I think you have to swear on something *you* own," Maureen pointed out.

"Okay, well . . ." I held up the Ziploc bag of left-over treats Mrs. Shepherd had foisted on me. "I swear on my Conrad Birdie Bundt cake."

Maureen's lips twitched, and a giggle slipped out. "In that case, I have to believe you."

When I got out to the car, I tossed my sleeping bag into the back, then slipped in next to my mother. "So?" she asked. "Was it as horrible as you thought it would be?"

I scowled. "Worse."

Okay, so that was a lie.

So maybe it was kind of the opposite of horrible. At least once we got past the whole I-hate-you I-hate-you-more part of the night. Not that Maureen and I were friends or anything. I didn't know what we were. But we weren't enemies anymore. Which meant my mom had been right all along.

And there was no way I was telling her *that*.

☆ *Chapter 7* ☆

"Remember," Ms. Hedley announced on Monday as we finished our opening Circle of Energy, "you're not just a cast, you're a *family*." Then she sent the chorus offstage to watch the principals rehearse their solos.

"If this cast is a family, I guess we're the great-great-stepnephew-twice-removed that everyone forgets to invite to Thanksgiving dinner," Kayla grumbled. She dropped into one of the auditorium seats and kicked her legs up on the chair in front of her. Onstage, Anoop and Maureen practiced the waltz they would dance as their characters (a vicious vampire and the innocent maiden) fell in love. A tinny recording of the music — a love song called "My Heart Drinks Your Blood" — played in the background.

"All hail the vampire king and his lovely queen," Kayla murmured, saluting the stage. "I bet Maureen can't wait until she gets her hands on her costume. She'll probably wear her crown all over school."

I winced. "Come on," I said. "She's not so bad."

Just then, Maureen stumbled over Anoop's big feet and almost fell.

Kayla giggled. "She's not so good either."

"You guys have a lot of stuff in common."

Kayla whirled around to stare at me. "*Excuse* me?" she said in exaggerated shock. "Since when do you know anything about Maureen Shepherd? Other than that she hates you and did her best to embarrass you in front of the whole school?"

Ms. Hedley shot us a sharp glance. Kayla lowered her voice. "Or have you forgotten the Festival of Humiliation?"

"She says she didn't do that," I said.

"And you *believe* her?"

"Yeah, I guess so. I know what she's like at school, but at her house this weekend —"

"Wait." Kayla tensed. "You went to her sleepover? I thought you weren't invited."

"I wasn't," I said. "Her mom invited me at the last minute, and *my* mom made me go, and we actually had a lot of fun —" I stopped when I saw

107

the look on Kayla's face. Her lips were pressed tight together, and she was holding her head very, very still. "What?"

Kayla slouched down in the chair. "Nothing. I just didn't think . . . never mind."

"What is it?"

"So you guys are, like, friends now?" she asked.

Something suddenly hit me: Was she *jealous*?

"I don't think so." This whole friend thing was so confusing. There should be membership cards. "But maybe we *could* be friends, you know? If we wanted to be."

"Yeah." She slouched even lower in her seat. "Figures."

"What figures?"

"You and Maureen. It's so obvious. You're both star material, right? You've both got that — what do you always call it?"

"Star presence," I said quietly.

"Yeah. Some people are destined to be stars and other people are destined to be in the *chorus*. You belong up there," Kayla said, nodding at the stage. "Not down here, with me."

I know it's horrible, but a tiny bit of me was excited that Kayla was jealous. Because that meant she wanted to be friends with me as much as I wanted to be friends with her.

"This is where I belong," I said firmly. And I honestly believed it. I started humming quietly, just loud enough that Kayla could hear me. I knew it was one of her favorite songs.

She rolled her eyes at me. "Stop it."

But instead I hummed a little louder, doing a silly head bop in time with the music. Then I started to sing. "*Wherever we go . . .*"

I could tell she wanted to smile.

"*Whatever we do . . .*"

"This is ridiculous," she complained.

"Come on," I urged her. "It's Sondheim. Your favorite . . ."

"Which is why I won't massacre the song by singing it in my horrible, horrible voice."

"*We're gonna go through it —*"

"*Together!*" She joined in with me, loud and clear. I knew she couldn't resist. We sang the next few lines — until suddenly, we realized that everyone was staring at us.

"Dude, no one told me to bring earplugs to school!" Anoop called out.

"I think what Anoop *means* is that it's always gratifying to see theatrical eagerness in members of the *Monster Mash* family," the director said, peering down at us. "But perhaps while we're trying to rehearse, the two of you might consider being just a little less eager?"

"Yes, Ms. Hedley," we mumbled.

"Maybe you can expend some of that excess energy on an errand. Can you run backstage and see whether the set for the zombie salsa scene is ready? And feel free to go" — she raised her eyebrows — *"together."*

We did.

Here's the thing about being in the chorus, at least at Alencia Valley Middle School: There wasn't that much to do. Sure, there were lyrics and dance moves to learn, but Ms. Hedley must have figured we could do that on our own, because she spent most of her time with the principals. We were stuck in rehearsal for almost two hours a day — and for most of those hours, we weren't doing anything.

At least, not anything official.

When I was on tour, I always wondered what the chorus did while I was rehearsing. I saw them sometimes, sprawled out in the back of the theater or off in the wings, gossiping and laughing and eating pizza. No one ever offered me a slice. Even when I had a pretty small part, they never treated me like I was one of them. I was always just *the kid.* I thought it might be different when I was Annie in *Annie* . . . but it was worse. We were all kids, but we weren't all the same. I was the star and they weren't.

I guess I'll never know what they were doing to fill up all their free time, but I know what the *Monster Mash* chorus was doing: playing cards. That wasn't *all* we did, of course — we flipped through cheesy magazines, tested ourselves on Broadway trivia, recapped bad TV shows, gossiped about terrible teachers and annoying parents, swapped music, played games on our cell phones, and — oh yeah — every once in a while we rehearsed.

But mostly we played cards. I wasn't very good at hearts or gin rummy, but I was *really* good at slap spit. It was a two-person game, sort of like speed solitaire. At the end, you had to slam your palm down on the smallest pile of cards before your opponent did. It was my favorite part. I pictured Jerry the producer's face on the top card, saying, "You're fired."

I always slapped first. And I always slapped hardest.

"Bored now," Kayla chirped as I won my third game in a row.

It was one week after Maureen's sleepover, two

weeks before opening night — and even slap spit was getting old.

"There's got to be something else we can do." Kayla turned to Sam and Jaida. "Remember what we used to do last year?"

Sam's smile widened. "*Excellent*. Jaida, do you still have —"

"It's in my locker." Jaida rubbed her hands together like a supervillain. "We should go now, while Ms. Hedley's not paying attention."

"Um, go where?" I asked.

Kayla winked. "You'll see." She turned to Sam and Jaida. "We'll meet you guys there." She tugged me toward the bathroom.

"Seriously, where are we going?" I asked again, pausing at the door. "Ms. Hedley will go nuts if she realizes we snuck out of rehearsal."

"She's *already* nuts," Kayla pointed out. "And besides, she's not going to find out."

We were about to go into the bathroom when we heard Lee 'n' Lee inside. Their voices floated out through the thin door.

"She thinks she's so great," one of the Lees complained. It was probably Emily. She had a very slight lisp.

"We just have to be nice to her for a little

longer. You know she's got Hedley wrapped around her little finger," Natalie said. "We can ditch her again when the show's over."

Emily snickered. "When's she going to notice that we're only nice to her so we can get better parts?"

"Maybe when she notices that she's not the center of the universe?" Natalie suggested. "In other words, never." They burst into laughter.

They didn't have to say who *she* was — I knew they were talking about Maureen.

It was the Moment of Truth. If I'd been a character in a play, the stage would have gone dark, and the audience would have spent intermission trying to figure out what my character should do: Pretend I hadn't heard, or bust into the bathroom and tell them to stop.

Too bad life doesn't have intermissions, just bathroom breaks. I turned to Kayla, but she was already pushing her way inside.

"You two do realize that you just officially achieved the title of World's Worst Friends, right?" Kayla snapped at Lee 'n' Lee. They gaped at her in the mirror, shocked.

Not as shocked as me. Kayla was actually *defending* Maureen?

"Could you be any more obnoxious and pathetic, pretending to be friends with someone just to get a good part?"

"At least we *have* parts," Natalie sneered. "I'd rather be obnoxious than be in the chorus."

"Then congratulations," Kayla shot back. "You've succeeded beyond your wildest dreams." She stormed out of the room while Natalie was still trying to figure out what she meant.

"What was that?" I asked, once we were safely in the hallway. "I thought Maureen was your nemesis."

"I don't care what she is. No one deserves to be treated like that." Kayla grimaced. "I'm not saying I like her or anything."

"Of course not."

"I mean, I know *you* like her, and it's not like you have the worst taste in the world, so maybe, just *maybe* she's not as bad as I thought. . . ."

"Nice to see you've got an open mind," I teased.

"But this isn't about her," Kayla said. "It's about them." She jerked a thumb toward the bathroom door.

"Forget about them," I suggested. "Take me wherever it is we were going before they opened their big mouths."

"I thought you were worried about getting caught."

"Maybe I trust you," I said, and she smiled. "Or maybe I'm just *really* bored."

We decided to hit the bathroom by the cafeteria instead, then crept through the empty hallways to meet Jaida and Sam at the rendezvous point. This turned out to be Jaida's locker, at the far end of the science wing. She was holding a bright orange Frisbee.

"No way," I said.

Kayla nodded. "Yes way." And then she took off running down the long, narrow hallway. "I'm open!" she shouted. Jaida flung the Frisbee into the air. Kayla leaped up and caught it on her fingertips, then whipped it back toward us. I lunged for it without thinking, and it smacked into my open palm.

"Someone's going to hear us," I said nervously, tossing the Frisbee to Jaida. It sailed over her head, but she jumped up, stretching her arms high, and snatched it out of the air. Then she spiked it to the floor like she had scored a touchdown, and did a victory dance.

"Who's going to hear, Mr. Fulton?" Sam asked, referring to the ninety-two-year-old biology teacher famous for falling asleep in the middle of his classes (and sometimes in the middle of his sentences). "The last time he heard anything was during the Civil War."

"No one ever comes to this side of the school after hours," Kayla assured me. "Relax."

So I did. We raced up and down the hall, tossing the Frisbee back and forth — or trying to, at least. (Most times I threw the Frisbee, it went wild and clattered into a bank of lockers.) When we got tired of catch, we played a little monkey in the middle, and then tried to put together a game of ultimate, but none of us were quite sure of the rules. We leaped and jumped and stumbled and slammed into each other and, most of all, laughed. By the time we collapsed to the floor, our backs against the lockers, our legs sore, our chests heaving with giggles, and our fingers Frisbee-chapped, almost an hour had passed.

"Rehearsal's almost over — we should probably get back," Jaida said.

"That would be an excellent point," Sam agreed, still trying to catch his breath, "if I weren't too tired to move."

I was pretty sure that by now, even clueless Ms. Hedley had noticed we were gone, but I didn't care. If we got in trouble, it had been worth it.

Eventually, we pulled ourselves off the floor and stashed the Frisbee back in Jaida's locker. Then the four of us linked arms and did a *Wizard of Oz* shuffle back to the theater. *"We're off to our rehearsal,"* Kayla sang loudly in her horrible off-key voice, *"the most boring rehearsal of all. Because, because, because, because, becaaaaaaause, because Ms. Hedley's afraid we're klutzes who'll trip and fall."*

It was so strange wandering through the empty hallways. During school hours, Alencia Valley Middle School was pure misery, crowded with noise and smells that made you want to shut yourself in a locker just to get away. During school, the building belonged to other people: the teachers, who were always telling you what to do and where to go. The jocks, barging through the crowds without noticing or caring who they pushed. The popular kids, who made sure everyone knew that *they* were in and *you* were out. The kids who set off stink bombs and dumped milk on people's heads.

But after hours, the school belonged to us. We were on our own, with no one to tell us we were in the wrong place, wearing the wrong clothes, or that we weren't invited. There was no one to see us, so we didn't have to act. We could just be.

And from the look on Ms. Hedley's face when she spotted us slipping back into the theater, we were about to *be* in big trouble.

"You!" She glared down at our formerly merry foursome from the stage. I realized the theater was almost empty. It must have been even later than we'd thought. "I've been looking for you everywhere. We rehearsed 'March of the Undead,' and you missed it! And now you've missed our Circle of Energy!" She shook her head. "I expected better from you — especially you, Ruby. I thought someone with your experience would understand that being part of a cast carries with it a certain responsibility. I have to ask myself whether you truly want to appear in this production. . . ."

Ms. Hedley droned on, but I could barely hear her over the roaring in my ears. What if she threw us out of the show? Everything good in my life in Alencia came from being in *Monster Mash*. There was no way I could survive the whole normal-middle-schooler thing without it. But just when it seemed all hope was lost . . .

. . . enter Maureen, stage left. "It's my fault."

"*Your* fault?" Ms. Hedley echoed.

"Starring Maureen Shepherd, in the unlikely role of Our Hero," Kayla murmured.

I elbowed her in the side. "Shhh!"

"I don't see how," Ms. Hedley told Maureen. "*You* didn't disappear in the middle of rehearsal. In fact, *you* agreed to stay later with me for additional practice on your solos. That's the kind of commitment I'm looking for."

Maureen hesitated. "I asked them to run an errand for me," she blurted out. "I, uh, left my science book in my locker, and I need it to study, and my mom's picking me up as soon as we're done here, so I knew I wouldn't have time to get it myself. . . ." She gave Ms. Hedley a pleading look. "Blame me, not them."

"Oh. Well." Ms. Hedley's mouth soundlessly opened and closed a few times, goldfish-style. "That's different. Admirable work ethic, Maureen. And Ruby, it's lovely that you and your friends understand the demands of Maureen's part and were willing to help out. Her rehearsal time really is crucial. I suppose I owe you an apology, but . . ." She turned back to Maureen. "Why did you send *four* of them to collect one book?"

Maureen's eyes went wide. "Uh . . . I wasn't *sure* it was in my locker. So I sent Ruby to my locker, and Kayla checked the cafeteria, and Sam and

Jaida looked in the classroom and the, uh . . . locker room."

"We couldn't find it anywhere," I piped up. Kayla, Sam, and Jaida nodded eagerly, contorting their faces into something that was supposed to look like regret. "That's why it took us so long. We were looking and looking . . . sorry, Maureen." I gave her a weak smile.

"No problem. So, you're not mad?" Maureen asked Ms. Hedley.

"Of course not." Ms. Hedley patted her on the shoulder. "How could I be mad at my bright, shining star?"

Before she could change her mind, we collected our stuff in silence and went out to the parking lot to wait for our parents to pick us up. Kayla and I were still waiting when Maureen came outside.

"Thanks for doing that back there," Kayla mumbled, looking embarrassed. I realized I'd never actually seen her and Maureen speak to each other.

"Yeah, thank you *so* much," I added. "That was amazing."

Maureen shrugged. "No problem. So . . . what were you guys actually doing all that time?"

"You know," Kayla said. "Stuff."

"Playing Frisbee in the science wing," I said, grinning.

"Oh." Maureen got a weird look on her face. The same look that Kayla had when she found out I went to Maureen's sleepover. A look that said, *Not that I wanted to come . . . but it would've been nice to be invited.*

I remembered how I felt all those times on tour, when the chorus people went off somewhere and it didn't even occur to them to invite me along. I'd done the same thing to Maureen, without even realizing it. "Maybe next time, you could play, too," I said. Kayla shot me a what-are-you-*doing* look.

Maureen looked like she was deciding whether or not to smile.

She decided not.

"Thanks," she said. That smug tone was back, the one she'd always used on me before the sleepover. "But you heard Ms. Hedley. My rehearsal time is crucial. I guess that's what happens when you're the star."

Her mother pulled up to the curb, and Maureen climbed into the car without saying good-bye.

Kayla rolled her eyes at me. "I was *totally* wrong about her," she said sarcastically. "She's just lovely."

* * *

When I got home that night, there was an e-mail from Great-aunt Silva waiting for me, begging for details about life in Alencia. I wanted to write back — but what was I supposed to say? She wouldn't want to hear about sleepovers and Frisbee games. Was I supposed to tell her how relieved I was the first time Kayla invited me to sit at her lunch table, or how much more fun it was to do group work in French class when I wasn't in a group of one? (Even if group member number two was Maureen.)

If I told her all that, I knew how I'd sound: *normal.* And I knew exactly how Great-aunt Silva felt about normal.

As if that wasn't bad enough, I was in the chorus. Not that I was embarrassed or anything . . . not much, at least. But Great-aunt Silva was always so sure I would be a star. I was afraid she'd be disappointed.

Especially when she found out how much I was enjoying it.

So instead of e-mailing her back, I decided to work on my zombie costume. I would need a werewolf costume, too, but the zombie costume seemed slightly less impossible.

I figured I could just take some old jeans and a T-shirt and make them look all torn up and frayed.

Then maybe slap on some ketchup or paint to look like blood.

Unfortunately, when I tried on my newly zombified jeans, I didn't look much like a zombie. I looked more like I'd had a collision with a lawn mower and a jar of tomato sauce.

Figuring the zombie was a lost cause, I started brainstorming werewolf costume ideas. But they all required more materials (and more talent) than I had. I couldn't do anything about the talent problem, but I decided to hit up Alana's closet for some supplies. She was the artsy one in the family — or she used to be, back before she turned into a bratty, soccer-playing pod person. I figured she'd have to have something I could use.

And I was right: I found a sewing kit, three boxes of markers, and a basket of patterned fabric patches.

I also found a stack of posters with the lyrics of "On My Own" written across them.

"What are you doing in my closet?" Alana squeaked.

I whirled around, holding up the stack of posters — *my* posters. "What are *these* doing in your closet?"

"How should I know?" she asked in a panicky voice. "I guess you put them there."

"I can't believe you," I said in a low voice. It all made sense now. *Alana* had been at the French booth when I dropped off the posters. She would have had plenty of time to replace them with a new set. I wasn't even angry — well, okay, I was a little angry. But mostly I was stunned.

She dropped the act. "Look, I know it was stupid. But I never thought you'd actually take them onstage," she said quickly. "Why didn't you just *look* at them before you actually went out there?"

"So you're saying this is *my* fault?"

Alana shook her head. "What do you want me to say?"

"'Sorry' would be good," I said. "Not that you are."

"Am too!" she protested. "I told you, I didn't mean for it to happen. I mean, I guess I did, because I *did* it. But I'm sorry, okay? Can't we just call it even?"

Even for what? I wondered. What was she trying to get back at me for?

I guess I could have asked. But if I forced her to explain why she'd been mad at me, she might get mad all over again. At least she seemed honestly sorry.

That was a start.

"Fine," I said. "Call it even." I slipped past her, heading back to my bedroom to bury myself in hopeless costume-making.

"Wait," Alana said.

I paused in the doorway.

"What are you doing, anyway?" she asked hesitantly. "I mean, why'd you come in here?"

I sighed. "I was just looking for supplies. I'm *supposed* to be making myself a costume for the show . . . but it's kind of a disaster."

Alana smiled. "Remember when you tried to help me with my kindergarten Halloween costume?"

"I remember accidentally gluing Styrofoam to your hair," I said, giggling. "I thought Mom's head was going to explode."

"I thought she was going to have to cut all my hair off to get it out," Alana said. "Then *your* head would've exploded. I would have made sure of it."

"You should have been the one making *my* Halloween costume," I admitted. "You were always better at that stuff than me."

"A monkey would be better at that stuff than you." She pulled her hair out of its ponytail. It fell, smooth and glossy, down her shoulders. I still couldn't believe how different she was than the grungy little kid I remembered. "If you want, I could help you," she said slowly. "You know, with your costume."

I wrinkled my forehead. "I *definitely* want your help, but . . . really?"

"Why not?" she asked.

Maybe because you've been acting like me coming home somehow ruined your life? I thought. So you've been trying to ruin mine?

But I kept that one to myself.

"You seem pretty busy," I said, trying to sound casual. "With soccer and your friends and everything. I just thought maybe you wouldn't have time."

"I have time," she said.

If this was the old Alana, the giddy little kid with paint-smeared freckles and chocolate-smeared lips, I would have squeezed her into a hug. But the old Alana disappeared while I was in Paris — and I was just starting to figure out the new one.

"Okay," I said, staying where I was. "Cool."

"Yeah." She nodded. "Cool."

Chapter 8

When rehearsal ended the next day, Kayla and I were the first to take our seats for the Circle of Energy. After the Frisbee crisis, we were on our best behavior. We sat cross-legged, hands clasped, waiting for Ms. Hedley to begin her standard invocation.

Instead, she clapped her hands together. "Darlings, I have a thrilling announcement for you all. As many of you know, my husband, Dash Hedley, is an extremely talented actor — and he's just been offered a part in a major motion picture!"

She beamed at us expectantly.

"Uh, congratulations?" Maureen offered.

Ms. Hedley's smile stretched even wider. "It'll be a three-month shoot in Arizona. The best news of all is that I'll be joining him on the set, tutoring some of the younger actors. I might even appear in the movie myself!"

"Congratulations!" Lee 'n' Lee chorused.

"Of course, I'm just *devastated* to leave you in the lurch like this, but you're all so talented and utterly brilliant that I know you'll persevere. You know what they say about the *thee-ate-or*: The show must go on!"

Maureen half raised her hand. "When you say you're leaving, what do you mean?"

Ms. Hedley lightly tapped herself on the ear. "For a good actor, listening is as important as speaking."

Maureen flushed. "I *was* listening," she protested. "I just didn't —"

"*When* are you leaving, Ms. Hedley?" I cut in.

"Why, tomorrow," she said. "We head out for Arizona first thing in the morning. So I'm afraid this is our last day together, cast."

"But the show's in two weeks!" Kayla exclaimed. "What are we supposed to do without you?"

I knew how she felt. Ms. Hedley was a flake — but she was still our director. We needed her.

"Have no fear, darlings. Would I leave my favorite thespians to fend for themselves?"

Apparently, yes.

"Of course not!" She tittered, but the laugh sounded pretty fake. "The school has assigned Mr. Amato to take over once I'm gone. He'll see you through opening night."

Gasps and murmurs rippled across the Circle of Energy. Anoop gagged dramatically.

"Who's Mr. Amato?" I whispered to Kayla.

"The boys' swim coach," she whispered back. "And he teaches gym and health. I mean, he 'teaches.'" She used her fingers to curl quote marks around the word.

"But he doesn't know anything about drama," Maureen protested loudly. She looked horrified. I remembered what she'd told me about Ms. Hedley at her sleepover. Kayla and her chorus friends might think the drama teacher was a weirdo, but Maureen saw her as the woman who could make her into a star. She was like Maureen's version of Great-aunt Silva . . . and she was about to disappear.

"True," Ms. Hedley admitted. "But I've spoken with him at length, and he's very eager to learn."

Kayla leaned toward me. "They had to close the pool this month for renovations, so I'm guessing he's just eager for something to do," she whispered. "Trust me, we're doomed."

"The show will go on, and I'm sure it will be

magnificent," Ms. Hedley said with forced brightness. "And as a little farewell treat . . ." She pulled a large cardboard box out from behind her back. "I brought doughnuts!"

The cast swarmed around the food.

"This is totally bogus," Anoop grumbled, stuffing his face with a chocolate cruller.

"Maybe it won't be so bad," Maddie Crayne said timidly. "After all, Ms. Hedley's kind of" — she lowered her voice — "flaky."

"You don't know Amato!" Anoop snapped. "He's — ah, forget it. I'm out of here, dude."

"What's his problem now?" Sam asked as Anoop stormed out of the theater. Jaida shrugged.

"It's Coach Amato," Mark Castle said. "I'm in his gym class, and Anoop is a total klutz."

"Um, is this supposed to be a surprise?" Kayla asked.

Jaida blushed. "He's not so bad. It's not like any of us are good dancers."

"It's not like any of us are the star of the play," Kayla countered.

"Anyway, Anoop's always messing up in gym class, and Amato likes to use him as an example of what *not* to do," Mark explained. "Having the guy show up here is probably his worst nightmare."

Sam flashed a wicked grin. "So maybe the news isn't all bad."

"Behave," Kayla said, smacking his shoulder. "We have bigger problems to deal with than Anoop's big head. Right, Ruby?"

"Um, yeah," I said. "Right."

But I was only half listening. Maureen had trapped Ms. Hedley in a corner, and I was trying to overhear their conversation.

"But you promised you were going to introduce me to your casting director friend," Maureen said. "And that next year I could be your assistant director!"

"I'm sorry, Maureen, but what can I say? The *thee-ate-or* is a harsh mistress."

"It's not the theater." Maureen wrinkled her nose. "It's the *movies*. You always said that the movie industry didn't have a soul. That only stage acting mattered."

"Well . . . I . . ." Ms. Hedley brushed her long hair away from her face. "You'll understand someday, when you get your big break." She gave Maureen a brusque pat on the back. "Good luck, dear."

And then, before the rest of the cast could notice she was leaving, she ducked out of the theater.

"My big break," Maureen muttered. "Like that's ever going to happen now."

"Maureen," I said hesitantly. "I'm sorry about Ms. Hedley."

She shrugged, tossing her hair so that the curls fell in front of her face. "It's not like you made her quit."

"We'll figure something out," I said, trying to sound encouraging. "She's right about one thing. The show must go on, right?"

"What do you even care?" she asked bitterly. "You're just passing through, right? Here until you get your next big part somewhere else. So don't pretend you care about this show or what happens to it."

"But I —"

"After all, it's not *real*," Maureen snapped. "When you get a better offer, you'll be out of here just as fast as Ms. Hedley. But for the rest of us, this is it. Get it?" she said angrily.

I didn't know what to say.

"Tell me I'm wrong," she challenged me. "That this isn't just some unwelcome break from your *real* life."

"I was just trying to help," I said. "I won't do it again."

"I guess that's your answer," she called as I walked away.

It wasn't. I hadn't given her an answer — because I didn't have one.

"And then she started blasting me like *I* was the one who was ruining everything," I complained, trying to sew the seams like Alana had showed me. We were sitting in the dining room, working on my costume. At least, Alana was working. I was mostly fuming. "Can you believe that?"

Alana didn't look up from the zombie mask she was painting.

"Well?" I said.

"What do you want me to say?" Her voice was so empty of emotion it almost sounded robotic.

"How about, 'I'm sorry you had such a bad day'?" I suggested. "Or, 'You'll figure something out, maybe this Amato guy isn't so bad.'"

Alana smirked. "Oh, he's bad. Kristin's older brother was on the swim team last year. He says the guy's totally incompetent. Though maybe he'll be better at theater than he is at swimming." She started giggling. "Couldn't be worse."

"You think this is *funny*?" I'd thought we'd finally moved past the whole Alana-hating-me thing.

"Am I supposed to feel sorry for you or something?"

"Well . . . yeah. Ms. Hedley didn't even give us any advance warning, it's just here one day, gone the next. It's like she expected us to be happy for her, even though she was totally ditching us."

Alana gave me a look of pure disdain. "You don't even see it, do you?"

Obviously not. "What?"

She shook her head, and dumped the costume stuff on the table. "Nothing. I've got homework to do."

"Alana, come on," I said. "What's going on?"

"You really don't get it, do you?" She hugged her arms to her chest. "You remember leaving for your first national tour?"

"*Mary Poppins*? Sure."

"What do you remember about the day you left?"

"It was my first time on an airplane," I said, smiling at the memory. "I was so excited I forgot to be scared. And Mom and Dad surprised me with a cell phone right before I got on the plane, so I could call them anytime."

"Anything else?"

"Maybe you should just tell me what I'm supposed to be remembering."

"Remember what *I* was doing?" she asked.

"You were . . ." I thought for a moment, then wrinkled my forehead. "You weren't even there. Where were you, anyway?"

"At my dance recital," she said. "Doing the solo you promised to help me rehearse. The one you were too busy to help with because you had a million things to do to get ready for the tour. The one Mom and Dad had to miss because they were taking *you* to the airport. Remember?"

I guess I could have lied, but something told me not to. "No."

"Just like you probably don't remember that you promised to teach me how to swim that summer. Or that you promised we'd go to the amusement park and see if I was finally tall enough to ride the roller coaster. Or that you promised to talk your teacher into letting me be a Munchkin when your class put on *The Wizard of Oz*."

"I promised a lot of stuff, huh?" I didn't remember any of it.

"Yeah. You did. And then you just went away, and you never came back."

"I came back all the time!" I protested.

"For *vacation*," Alana said. "It's not the same. You probably didn't even miss me. You were having all these exciting adventures and I was stuck here, knowing my big sister had better things to do than hang out with me."

"Alana — I didn't know. I didn't even think about that."

"That's kind of the point," she snapped. "Forget it." She waved her hand, shooing away her complaints.

"I *did* miss you," I said after a minute. "All the time. For the first few weeks on tour, I used to cry myself to sleep. I almost asked Great-aunt Silva to take me back to the airport and send me home."

"Really?" She looked suspicious. "How come I never heard about that?"

"Because I didn't tell anyone," I said. "Mom and Dad were so excited for me when I got the part, and they seemed so proud . . . I just wanted to prove that I could handle it, you know? But half the time, I just wanted to come back here and ride roller coasters with you."

Alana looked down, grinding her toe into the carpet. "But that changed. You don't want to be here anymore. Mom's forcing you. If you had your way, you'd leave tomorrow."

"That's not true."

136

She gave me a skeptical look.

"I mean, that *was* true," I quickly corrected myself. "But not now. Being home's not so bad." There was the show (unless it all fell apart without Ms. Hedley), there was Kayla (who was probably-definitely-almost an official friend), there was Maureen (before she randomly decided we were enemies again), and (when she was speaking to me, as opposed to ignoring me or yelling at me) Alana.

Not to mention my own room and — even though it didn't taste very good — my parents' home cooking.

Oh, and my parents. When they weren't annoying me.

"You'd be out of here in a second if you got the chance," Alana argued.

"Look, I can't promise you that I'm never leaving again. But you heard Mom — I'm here for the rest of the year, at least. That's something, right? Enough time to ride some roller coasters, anyway."

Alana rolled her eyes. "I'm a little old for that now, don't you think?"

"You're in *fifth grade*!" I sputtered. "How can you be too old for roller coasters? *I'm* not too old for roller coasters."

Alana gave me her best bratty-little-sister smile. "I guess I'm just more mature than you."

I tossed a pillow at her, and she batted it out of the way just in time. "See?" she gloated. "Definitely more mature."

"That's why you need me around," I said. "To keep you young at heart. How about tomorrow night we gorge ourselves on popcorn and bad cartoons, like we used to?"

Alana shook her head.

So this is it, I thought. I'd turned my little sister against me, and nothing I could say would change her mind.

"Mom's taking me to the mall tomorrow night," she said. "I need new soccer cleats."

"Yeah, what is it with you and *soccer*?" I asked. "Since when do members of this family play sports?"

"Maybe I'm starting a new family tradition." She swung her leg through the air, kicking an invisible ball. "Besides, it's fun to kick stuff."

Now *that* sounded like the Alana I remembered.

"Why don't I go to the mall with you and help you pick out some sneakers?" I suggested.

"Cleats."

"Whatever. Then we could grab some cinnamon-swirl ice cream at Mr. Freeze," I said, hoping to tempt her into it. "Your favorite."

"Mr. Freeze closed last year," she said. "And cinnamon-swirl is gross."

Oh.

"But the new smoothie place has excellent strawberry shakes," she added, just when I'd given up all hope.

"Perfect," I said. "So, tomorrow night?"

"Tomorrow night." Alana nodded, and her mouth curved up in a mischievous smile. "Your treat."

☆ *Chapter 9* ☆

"I've never directed a play before," Coach Amato informed us at rehearsal the next day. (Right after he informed us that we should call him *Coach*.) "But I've been to a few plays." He issued a hearty and obviously fake chuckle. "Mostly 'cause my wife made me."

The cast sat silent in the front couple rows of the auditorium, staring at the man who controlled our theatrical destiny. He was short and stocky, with a red face and spiky brown hair that almost disguised the bald spot on the back of his head — but not quite. He strutted awkwardly along the edge of the stage, a blank clipboard swinging by his side. There was a stopwatch hanging around his neck. I was afraid he was going to make us run timed heats back and forth across the stage.

"Ms. Hedley said you guys know what you're doing," Coach said, hopping off the stage and taking a seat in the audience. "So just, uh, keep doing what you're doing. If you've got any problems, I'll be here." He pulled out a newspaper.

None of us moved.

Even Anoop, who usually couldn't get through two minutes without shouting something dumb, was sitting very still. He'd slunk way down in his seat, like he was hoping Coach Amato wouldn't notice he was there.

Coach Amato raised his eyebrows, peering at us over his newspaper. "You can get started now."

There was another long, silent pause.

"Am I missing something?" he said. "Is there something I'm supposed to do to kick things off? Should I get my starting gun?" He chuckled loudly at his own lame joke. Was it possible he actually thought he was being funny? "You guys are the experts," he said. "You tell me."

"You're the director," Maureen said. "So you're supposed to, you know . . . direct."

"You guys really want *me* telling you how to put on your show?" Coach Amato asked, laughing again. "That'd be like Anoop here teaching one of my swimmers how to do the butterfly." Anoop scowled and slunk lower in his chair. "But, if you insist . . ." He waved a hand at the stage. "Head up there and, uh, rehearse the first period."

"First *act*," Maureen corrected him.

"Right," he said. "That."

We'd never tried a full run-through of the first act before, but we took our places and tried our best.

It wasn't pretty.

Anoop flubbed his opening line, which threw off Lee 'n' Lee, who missed their cue and were so flustered that they forgot all the steps to the "My Daddy's a Werewolf and My Momma's a Vampire" dance. "Zombie Dance Party" started off okay, even if half the chorus still couldn't sing and dance at the same time. But then Jaida tripped over Sam's foot and slammed into Anoop, who was supposed to be preparing for his "Vampire's Lament" on stage right. He wheeled his arms wildly, trying to keep his balance, and knocked into the freshly painted sets for "Baby, You Slay Me." They toppled over, smearing Anoop, Jaida, and Lee 'n' Lee with red paint.

"Watch where you're going!" Anoop yelled at Jaida, disentangling himself from the broken set.

"You're not even supposed to be on this side of the stage," Jaida protested.

"And you shouldn't be onstage at all," Anoop shot back. "You're a total klutz."

Sam turned red. "You're calling *her* a klutz?"

"She's making me look bad!"

"Trust me, you don't need her help for that," Sam said. "*You're* the klutz."

Anoop glanced at Coach Amato, who was ignoring the whole thing. "I'm no klutz!"

"Enough!" Maureen shouted, her voice echoing across the stage. "Everyone stop, *now*!"

We all froze.

Out in the audience, Coach Amato even put down his newspaper long enough to make sure there were no gushing wounds or broken bones. Then he disappeared behind the sports section again.

Maureen ran her hands through her wavy hair. She marched to the edge of the stage and faced the cast, hands on her hips. "Principals on stage right," she ordered. "Chorus, stage left."

Everyone obeyed, including me.

"Okay." Maureen sucked in her lips for a moment, then blew out all her breath in an exasperated burst. She pointed at the chorus. "You guys practice the choreography for 'Zombie Dance Party.' It's a disaster." All around me, kids started muttering. "Ruby's in charge. Fix it."

143

Wait, *who's* in charge? I thought. But before I could object, Maureen turned to the principals, including paint-smudged Anoop. "You guys come with me. We'll run through scenes two to five, then meet up with the chorus to run through the opening again. That is" — Maureen raised her eyebrows at Coach Amato — "if it's okay with you. *Coach.*"

He waved an arm at her, not even bothering to peek out over his paper. "Sounds great. Uh, *action!*"

"Who does she think she is?" one of the chorus kids grumbled as we took our places for "Zombie Dance Party."

"Someone who actually knows what she's talking about?" Kayla retorted.

That was the last complaint, at least until we started running through the number. Ms. Hedley had choreographed it herself — which was the problem. Basically, we stood in three rows, sashaying back and forth from one side of the stage to the other, doing these lame hand motions in sync. Arms up, arms down, arms out, arms down, arms up, arms shake, arms down. You get the idea.

It wasn't neuroscience. It wasn't even technically *dancing*. But still, half the people needed to count out loud to figure out where their arms were supposed to be. They kept bumping into whoever was unfortunate enough to be next to them in line. Or sashaying left when they were supposed to go right, and knocking down half the row.

After the third time this happened, there was a mutiny.

"Maureen's right, this is a total disaster," Sam said, plopping to the floor.

"We look like a bunch of spastic robots, not zombies," Shayna complained, dropping down beside him. Soon, everyone was sitting down and whining.

"This is hopeless."

"And it's not our fault."

"Even if we knew what we were doing, we'd still look crazy. This dance is capital *L* lame."

Maureen had put me in charge, but I didn't know what I was supposed to do. On tour, you did what the director told you to do, or you got fired. (Of course, sometimes you got fired anyway just for growing a couple inches, but that was beside the point.) You didn't just quit in the middle of the rehearsal or ignore your director, even when your director was a middle-aged swim coach who probably would have been happy to leave an orangutan in charge, if it gave him more time to read the paper. And if he could get his hands on an orangutan.

Kayla jumped up and threaded her way through the chorus members until she was standing at the front of the crowd. "Look, we all hate this dance, right?"

Everyone nodded, including me.

"When Ms. Hedley was in charge, we had to do what she said, lame or not. But she's gone. So if we don't like the dance, we should do something about it."

"Like what?" Jaida asked.

"Like make up a new one." Kayla grinned. She turned to me. "You know the big disco scene in the movie version of *Bell-bottom Summer*?"

"Yeah . . ." I pictured the scene in my head. The chorus was about the same size as ours, dancing across the same type of space, the steps were simple, and the music tempo was the same. Of course, we'd have to switch a few things around, but Kayla was right. It could work. And it was definitely better than what we had. "But I haven't seen that movie in a couple years. I don't remember the steps exactly," I said.

"I do," Kayla assured me. "I'll show you, and then you'll show everyone else."

"Why me?"

"Because I dance about as well as I sing — I may know what it's supposed to look like, but that doesn't mean I can do it myself. You're the expert, right? You've taken classes with world-famous choreographers. Don't you think she knows what she's doing?" she asked the chorus. Everyone nodded or shouted yes — even the people who had never spoken to me. "See?" Kayla smirked, laughter in her eyes. "And besides, let's not forget — Maureen left you in charge."

Making up a new dance two weeks before show-time without the help of a professional choreographer or any kind of a director, with a chorus full of kids who could barely walk up the stairs without falling? It could have been a huge mistake.

It *should* have been a huge mistake.

But somehow, by the time an hour had passed, we were actually dancing in sync. We even managed to do one full run-through without anyone falling down!

"Is it just me, or is this actually working?" I

murmured to Kayla as we led the chorus through the number again.

"Forget it!" The shout came from the back of the theater. Anoop stormed out of the darkness, shaking his head. "No way."

Maureen chased after him. "It was just a suggestion," she called out. "Since your voice keeps cracking —"

"I said *forget it*!" Anoop's face was bright red. He slung his backpack over his shoulder. "I'm out of here. How are we supposed to put on a show like this?" He shook his head. "We're not ready, we're not going to *get* ready. Maybe the rest of you want to look like idiots in front of the whole school, but I'm out."

"You're quitting?" Maureen paled. "You can't quit!"

"Watch me," Anoop said. "And if the rest of you are smart, you'll drop out, too."

"Maybe he's right," Emily said, nudging Natalie.

"Yeah," Natalie said. "Maybe we should just cancel the show this year."

Cancel the show?

"Are you *insane*?" Maureen said. "We can't cancel the show. Mr. Amato —"

"*Coach* Amato," he corrected her, peeking over the top of his paper.

"Coach Amato, tell them we can't just cancel the show. The show must go on, right? That's, like, a rule of the theater."

The coach shrugged. "It may be a rule of the theater, but it's not a rule of the school, as far as I know. They told me I had to sit here and make sure you guys didn't kill each other, but they didn't say anything about the show must go on. We're all adults here, right?"

Um, no.

"I can't *force* anyone to be in the show," he told Maureen. "That'd be like me forcing you to join the swim team — then throwing you in the pool with all your clothes on." Another fake-sounding belly laugh. "You wouldn't like that much, would you?"

Maureen looked like she didn't like much of anything at the moment — especially Coach Amato.

"Maybe we should just slow down," I said loudly.

Everyone looked at me, waiting to see what I meant. The problem was, I wasn't sure. I hadn't even intended to say anything. But once I did, there wasn't much choice. I was in the spotlight — and that was the one place where I was supposed to know exactly what to do.

"The show's not for another two weeks, right?" I continued. "So even if we decide to cancel it —" Maureen glared at me. "Even *if*, we don't have to do it today, right?"

"I'm not wasting my time with rehearsals if we're just going to cancel at the last minute," someone in the crowd complained.

"I'm not saying we wait until the last minute," I said. "I'm just saying we should think about this before we do anything crazy, right?"

Anoop scowled. "*Crazy* is humiliating ourselves in front of the whole school."

"But what if we could come up with a way to make sure this show was the best Alencia's ever seen?" I argued. "And you were the star?" Maureen glared at me again. "*Co*star," I added quickly.

He looked thoughtful. Maybe because he knew the drama kids (drama *girls*) only liked him because he was always the star (*co*star) of the plays.

"You've got a way to do that?" he asked doubtfully.

"Not yet," I admitted. "But if we had more time . . ."

"We'll come back tomorrow," Anoop said. Suddenly, he was the spokesperson for the quit-the-show movement. "And you can give us a reason to stay. Or not."

He walked off the stage. Lee 'n' Lee scurried behind him, brushing past Maureen without a word. The rest of the cast drifted away, and Coach Amato must have figured that was his cue, because he ducked out, too. Soon only Maureen, Kayla, and I were left.

"That was pretty impressive," Kayla said, looking at me like she'd never seen me before.

"What?"

"First you whip the chorus into shape —"

"That was your idea," I pointed out.

"But *your* execution," she argued. "Then you talk our very own Conrad Birdie out of flying away?"

"I bought us one extra day," I said. "That's not much." But I couldn't help feeling a little proud of myself. I'd spent so many years doing what someone else told me to do — dance like this, sing like this, act like this, move like this — I was a little surprised to find that I could direct myself.

"That's nothing," Maureen said sullenly. "Anoop's just going to quit tomorrow. And everyone else is going to quit with him. The show is ruined."

"Maybe not," Kayla said, looking thoughtful. "You ever see that old Judy Garland, Mickey Rooney movie *Babes in Arms*?"

Maureen and I shook our heads.

"It's really old, from the thirties or something," Kayla explained. "It's probably the most famous Judy/Mickey musical, although I think it's a little overrated and — fun fact, it came out the same year as *The Wizard of Oz*, and the woman who plays —"

"Can you stop trying to prove that you know more than we do and just tell us what you're talking about?" Maureen snapped.

"She's not trying to prove anything," I explained. "This is just how she thinks. For Kayla, the whole world's one big musical."

Kayla shrugged, as if to say, *Doesn't everyone think that way*?

"Of course," I said, giving Kayla a pointed look, "sometimes she gets a little carried away."

"Oh. Right." Kayla cleared her throat. "Look, the movie's about these kids who save the day by putting on a show in the town barn. No one thinks they can do it, because they're just kids, but they know everything about the theater, and, you know, they're Judy Garland and Mickey Rooney, so of course everyone lives happily ever after."

"But this isn't a movie," Maureen pointed out.

"That doesn't mean it can't have a happy ending," Kayla said. "Ruby knows everything about what it takes to put on a good show."

I blushed. "I wouldn't say I know *everything* —"

"And Maureen, you love bossing people around," Kayla continued.

Maureen nodded firmly. "True."

"And I'm an expert on anything and everything Broadway," Kayla said. "If it ever happened in the history of the musical, I know about it — that's got to count for something."

"You think we don't need Ms. Hedley," I said.

"We *definitely* don't need Coach Amato," Maureen added.

Kayla grinned. "I'm pretty sure even Coach would agree: Right now, all we need is a game plan."

My mom was happy to give me permission to go out on a school night. She was still dancing for joy at the idea I might actually have friends. So Kayla and I went back to Maureen's house to plot strategy. At least, we were supposed to plot strategy — until Kayla caught sight of Maureen's wall of playbills and the two of them spent the next hour comparing notes on their favorite shows. And the hour after that arguing about whether Sondheim was an "overrated atonal fraud" (Maureen), and if Richard Rodgers was a "cheeseball hack who threw his talent away to team up with Hammerstein" (Kayla). "I like them both," I said at one point — and was totally ignored.

Somewhere in there, we also had pizza.

But in between the arguments and the food and a painfully off-key *Guys and Dolls* sing-along, we somehow managed to come up with a game plan. By the time I got home, I was totally exhausted, a little sick from all the pizza, and absolutely certain we could pull it off.

It felt pretty good — until I stepped through the front door and tripped over Alana's muddy soccer cleats. You know how they say your life flashes before your eyes when you're about to die? Well, when you're about to fall on your face thanks to your little sister's muddy soccer cleats, something else flashes before your eyes.

At least, it did in my case.

Before I even hit the floor, I remembered it all. Time slowed down as I flashed through our fight the night before, our plan to go to the mall to pick out new cleats, my promise that I wouldn't let

Alana down again. The look on her face that said she suspected I'd ditch her all over again.

Like I just did.

Time sped up again, and I crashed to the ground with a thud. It hurt, but not as much as I deserved. I pulled myself up and raced upstairs, then knocked on Alana's door. No answer.

"I know you're in there!" I shouted, banging harder on the door.

"Your psychic abilities must be on the fritz," my father said from behind me. "She went straight from the mall to her friend Sasha's house."

"Oh." I stopped banging.

My father arched an eyebrow. "Problem?"

Obviously. But not the kind he could fix. I shook my head and mumbled good night, then slipped into my room and shut the door behind me. There was a note taped inside. It wasn't signed, but I recognized Alana's scrawl.

Thanks, sis, it read. I could almost hear her angry, sarcastic voice.

You're always here when I need you.

☆ *Chapter 10* ☆

Diva rule #10: *"Always give them the old fire, even when you feel like a squashed cake of ice."*
— Ethel Merman
(star of *Annie Get Your Gun*)

"We don't need Ms. Hedley," Maureen announced to the cast the next day. "And we don't need Coach Amato." He didn't even look up at the sound of his name. "Ruby's a professional — she knows how to get a show from rehearsal to opening night. And Kayla knows everything there is to know about musicals, period." Kayla and I were standing center stage, right next to Maureen. Each of us took a funny little bow.

"That's great, dude," Anoop shouted. "But what do *you* know?"

"I know we can do this, *dude*," Maureen said, glaring at him. "And I know that I worked too hard on this show just to walk away. I know *I'm* not scared to see it through."

156

Anoop jumped to his feet. "Who said anything about being scared? I'm no chicken!"

"You're no actor either," I shot back. "Not if you're willing to quit in the middle of a show."

Lee 'n' Lee gaped at me like I was insane for insulting him. The rest of the cast looked uncertain. They'd heard our pitch about how we could handle rehearsals on our own. They knew we were ready to work hard and do whatever it took to get the show on track. But we couldn't do it without them.

"We can't do it without you, Anoop," I added, giving him a simpering smile. I was tempted to tell him exactly what I thought of him . . . but then I had a better idea. "If you quit, there'll be no point in going forward. You're our leading man. Every girl in my homeroom is already planning to buy tickets, just so they can see you onstage. So, if you quit . . ."

Anoop narrowed his eyes. "Who said anything about quitting?" he said. "Let's do this thing."

If life were a movie, here's where the musical montage would start. You know, those scenes where they dial down the dialogue and amp up the triumphant music, and then the characters fall in love, or get in shape, or go to war, or win the game, all in the space of a few minutes?

Well, sometimes that's how it feels in real life. You're too stressed and too busy to notice the time passing, but every once in a while, you look up and realize you're really *doing it*. (Whatever it is.) And you can almost hear the music swell in the background, and imagine the camera closing in on your determined face.

So, okay, imagine the camera closing in on my face.

Imagine the music swelling — something like "There's No Business Like Show Business," or maybe the "Theme from Rocky."

And now imagine a whole jumble of scenes mashed up together, as the clock ticks down to opening night.

There's the scene where the entire cast decided to agree with Anoop. (This scene is called "Why Don't People Think for Themselves?") As soon as he voted *yes* to sticking with the show, everyone else was in, too. And suddenly we were all jumping around onstage and shouting about how it was going to be the greatest thing to hit Alencia Middle School since the cafeteria introduced Fro-Yo Fridays.

There's the "Can't We All Just Get Along?"

scene, the music swelling just as Anoop and Sam crash into each other, collapse into a tangled heap, ball up their fists . . . then burst into laughter and help each other up.

Then there are all the hard work scenes. (These are called "I'm Tired!" and "I'm Hungry!" and "Ouch, Stop Stepping on My Foot!") We rehearsed before school. We rehearsed after school. We even rehearsed during school, if you counted the day Maureen and I performed our *Zombies en Français* skit in French class. (Even Madame Johnson was impressed.) Thanks to her freakish movie memory, Kayla came up with new dances for half the chorus scenes. Soon, no one was bumping into each other anymore. (Although Anoop still couldn't tell his right from his left.)

Maureen was having a blast telling everyone what to do. She had a tough time keeping her mother away from rehearsals, but somehow she managed it. "If she finds out about this, she'll want to direct the thing herself," Maureen had warned us. After having met Mrs. Shepherd, I could believe it.

As for me, I spent most of my rehearsals backstage, coordinating with the tech crew — the stage managers and the set designers and the lighting and sound people. It seemed like every day, they had a million new questions. And, since I had spent pretty much my whole life hanging out backstage, it turned out I had the answers.

Cut to me figuring out that we needed to fix the angle of the tower set so it wouldn't throw the whole stage into shadow.

Cut to me showing the lighting people how to adjust the spotlight to highlight the new dance routines.

Cut to our first dress rehearsal, when I debuted my homemade werewolf costume in all its anti-glory. Alana was still giving me the silent treatment, so I had torn-up strips of brown T-shirt wrapped around my hands (fur), brown face-paint smeared across my chin (more fur), and two cardboard triangles sticking up from my head (ears). I pretty much got laughed off the stage.

Actually, you know what? Let's cut away from that.

Instead, there's me approving new fake fangs for our vampires . . . and fixing the onstage tape marks so no one would get confused about where they were supposed to stand . . . and working with the pit orchestra to figure out how we could get the singing and music to actually match up . . . and, well, you get the idea.

Now, I'm not saying that I single-handedly saved the show.

No, seriously, I'm not saying that.

True, they couldn't have done it without me. But I couldn't have done it without them either.

Now is the moment in the musical montage where the music fades out a little, just enough so that you can hear the characters talk, because someone's about to have an Important Realization.

"I still don't know what we're going to do with 'Zombie Dance Party,'" Kayla confided, a couple days before opening night. "With it coming right after the 'Vampire Warriors' scene, there's just no way the whole chorus can get changed and move the scenery around in time."

"I was afraid of that," I said. We'd done okay in rehearsal, but once we added costumes and sets, it was obvious that there just wasn't enough time between the two big scenes.

"So why not move the scene?" Maureen suggested. "We can switch it with 'A Fang Through My Heart.'"

That was Maureen's big solo ballad. Her character dressed up as a werewolf so she could spy on the monsters' tower. That's when she ran into her true love, the vampire prince, and has to decide whether or not to stake him.

"We can't move 'A Fang Through My Heart,'" I argued. "You've got a huge part in 'Vampire Warriors.' There's no way you can get into costume and position in time to sing your solo in the next scene."

Kayla nodded. "She's right. You can't do the Warriors scene as Princess Isabella, then throw on your werewolf costume and get to the top of the tower to sing your solo. Even *you* can't make a costume change that fast."

Maureen looked thoughtful. "Maybe I don't have to. Ruby's not even in 'Vampire Warriors,' right?"

"So?" Kayla asked.

"So *she'd* have plenty of time to get ready for the next scene," Maureen said. "Lady Isabella's disguised as a werewolf for 'A Fang Through My Heart.' No one in the audience will notice if it's me behind the mask . . . or Ruby."

Kayla and I looked at each other, uncertain.

Maureen sighed. "Look, if we try to keep the scenes where they are, it's going to be a disaster. The chorus will never be ready in time, and Anoop will probably throw on the wrong costume, start singing the wrong song, and fall off the stage. If we do it my way, the show goes on. No one will ever know the difference." She smirked. "As long as Ruby gets herself a better werewolf costume."

I had to admit, it could work. But . . .

"You'd give me your solo?" I asked. "That's your favorite number."

"It's not about me," Maureen said. (Here's where the music rises. Get ready for the seriously Important Realization.) "It's about the show."

Here's the thing about musical montages: They skip over stuff.

Real life doesn't work that way. So I couldn't skip over the fact that my sister had stopped talking to me, no matter how many times I apologized. As far as Alana was concerned, I'd ditched her all over again.

After about the hundredth "I'm sorry," I finally figured out that wouldn't be enough. So after our final dress rehearsal, I asked my mom to take me to the mall.

"On the night before your big show?" she asked, surprised. "Don't you want to eat an early dinner, watch an old movie, and be in bed by nine?"

I shrugged. That was my usual preopening night ritual, and she was right, I did want to do that. But like Maureen said, it wasn't about me. (Not always, at least.)

Most of the money I got on tour went to pay my travel and living expenses, and the rest of it went straight into a college fund. But my parents let me keep a little for myself. That night, I spent it all.

I had a little help, of course. Dad gave me the specs I needed and Mom skipped her book club to drive me to the mall. But every show needs some good supporting actors. When I got home, I put the shopping bag in front of Alana's bedroom door. I didn't bother knocking, because I knew there was no way she'd answer. I just left a note:

Unless you plan on keeping up the silent treatment forever, you better get over this — because I'm not going anywhere.

Okay, so it wasn't a particularly mushy-gushy apology, but we weren't a particularly mushy-gushy family. I said what I needed to say. I just hoped it would be enough.

Chapter 11 ☆

When I woke up the next morning, it was still dark out. According to the neon green digits on the clock by my bed, it was five forty-five A.M. But I was more than just awake. I was wired. I felt like I was plugged into an electrical outlet, glowing as bright as the clock.

Opening night, I thought, staring up at the ceiling.

I never get stage fright, so it took me a minute to identify the weird, churning sensation in my gut. People are always talking about getting butterflies. These were more like killer bees. And every time I thought about the show, one of them stung me.

This wasn't just another show. In a weird way, it felt like my first show — or at least, the first one that was really *mine*.

My stomach growled. I wasn't sure if I was hungry or nauseous, but I decided to bet on hungry. Mostly because there was some leftover chocolate chip coffee cake in the kitchen. I eased open my door, hoping it wouldn't squeak and wake up the rest of the house.

Then I took a step out of the bedroom — and almost fell on my face.

Great, I thought sourly, catching myself on the door frame. You do realize "break a leg" is a saying, not a suggestion, right?

I'd tripped over a folded bundle of fabric resting against my door. It was my werewolf costume — except it wasn't the hideously lame costume I'd made for myself. It was a brown, furry-tailed jumpsuit and a werewolf mask that looked frighteningly real, right down to the bloody fangs. It was absolutely perfect, and there was only one person in the house who could have done it.

Break a leg, the note said. *And I (mostly) don't mean that literally.* — *A*

Backstage was crazy. We were using the orchestra room as our dressing room.

"Who gave you the flowers?" Emily asked Anoop, who was preening in front of the mirror, holding a bouquet of good-luck roses.

He shrugged, never taking his eyes off his own image. "Katie, I think. Or maybe Allie? Dude, who can keep track?"

Everywhere you looked, kids were wriggling into and out of monster costumes, warming up their voices, practicing their lines, applying makeup, trying not to freak out, totally freaking out — and, of course, playing cards.

It was chaos. As we filed onto the stage and took our places for the opening number, we could hear the pit orchestra tuning up, and the audience murmuring. Maureen, standing center stage, glanced over her shoulder and gave me a thumbs-up. Kayla grinned and raised her eyebrows. "What do you think?" she whispered. "*Phantom* or *Carrie*?"

That's *The Phantom of the Opera*, Broadway's longest-running show.

And *Carrie*, Broadway's most notorious, horrific, disastrous, total-humiliation-for-everyone-involved flop.

Before I could answer, the lights dimmed.

The curtain rose.

Showtime!

Spoiler alert: *Monster Mash: The Musical* was a hit. And I knew it would be, from the moment the spotlight hit us. Sure, Anoop went left when he should have gone right and collided with Jaida, but no one noticed. Sam's werewolf ears fell off midway into the first song, but he stayed in character, and managed to stick them back on when no one was looking. Kayla was completely off-key, as usual, but her voice disappeared amid everyone else's. That's the beauty of the chorus.

I could tell from the applause after our first scene: The audience belonged to us. There's just a feeling you get, when things are going really well, that the audience will follow you wherever you want to take them. That they're willing to forget that you're just a bunch of people jumping around onstage. They believe the story you're telling.

Maybe I belong in the chorus, I thought as I fell into step between Kayla and Sam, bouncing up and down in sync with my fellow werewolves. Or maybe I belong backstage. Not just playing cards and tossing a Frisbee, but coordinating set changes and solving prop crises (while Coach Amato hung out in the back of the orchestra room, watching football on his mini TV). Maybe I wasn't born to be a star after all.

Then I got up onstage to sing Maureen's solo.

And I knew that no matter how great all that

other stuff was, it didn't even come close to standing under the spotlight.

"*Blood on your fangs, a stake in my hand,*" I sang mournfully. "*I know I must strike, but I can't understand.*"

I forgot the audience in front of me, the wooden slats of the stage beneath me, the rickety sets wobbling over me. I forgot the blinding spotlight. The off-key orchestra. The fake fur of the mask scratching my face. I forgot everything but the music.

"*I know you're a vampire, but must you drink blood?*

And must my garlic keep us apart?

I know you're a vampire, but must you drink blood?

Staking you would only be

A fang through my heart."

For a moment, I *was* Lady Isabella, weeping for my vampire love. And then the song ended, and thundering applause echoed through the theater, and I was me again.

Ruby Day.

Born to be a star.

"Congratulations, Ruby!" Alana said, thrusting a bouquet of yellow daisies into my arms. Exhausted cast members and proud families swarmed all around us. My parents were still lost in the crowd somewhere, but Alana had battled her way through. "You looked awesome up there!"

"All thanks to your costume," I told her. "So I guess that means you forgive me?"

She lifted the cuff of her jeans to show me the new cleats she was wearing. Her shopping trip with Mom had been a big failure, since the cleats she wanted were too expensive. Lucky for Alana, I had a lot of money to spend and an angry little sister to impress. "What does that tell you?"

"It tells me I can buy your love," I teased.

"Then I guess I've finally got you well-trained," she shot back.

"So do the cleats replace the tiara? Are you going to wear them everywhere now?"

"No way!" She brushed off an imaginary speck of dirt. "After today, these aren't going anywhere but the field."

"Good," I said.

"What do you care?"

"Because now I can keep calling you the little princess." I laughed, finally feeling like I had my sister back again.

Suddenly, a familiar voice floated across the crowd. "*Dahling*, you were *très magnifique!*"

My eyes widened. "Great-aunt Silva?" I said in confusion as she swept me into a tight hug. "What are you doing here?"

"What *I* don't understand is why you didn't invite me yourself!" Great-aunt Silva replied. "To think, I almost missed your debut performance!"

I felt my cheeks heat up. "I know how much you hate it here," I said. "And, well, I guess I was kind of embarrassed about . . . being in the chorus."

Great-aunt Silva shook her head. "Lucky thing your parents have more smarts than you do," she said. "Otherwise, I would have missed your glorious performance. Ashamed of being in the chorus? Have I taught you nothing? What do I always say?"

"There are no small parts," I said dutifully. "Only small actors."

"Exactly!" Great-aunt Silva hugged me again. "And you're *no* small actor," she whispered furiously. "You're the biggest and best one I know."

It was so weird to see her in the school auditorium, next to my parents and my sister. Like discovering a little piece of Paris at the heart of Alencia. But it didn't make me miss Paris at all. It made me even happier to be home.

"Wait here," I told her. "You have to meet my friends."

Great-aunt Silva gave me a secretive smile. "I'd be happy to — and I've brought someone with me I think you'll be rather happy to see, as well."

"Who?" I couldn't even come up with a guess. Certainly not Jerry the producer — I'd be happy never to see him again. Maybe his assistant, Helen, had shown up, along with some (used) Dr. Seuss books?

"It's a surprise. But you're going to love it," Great-aunt Silva promised. "Now hurry off and find those friends. I want to make sure they're good enough for you."

I found my friends hiding behind a row of seats, peering over the top, shaking with laughter. "Do I even want to know what you guys are doing?"

Kayla pointed over to Anoop, who was a few feet away, talking to an old man who looked sort of like him. "You remember those flowers he got before the show?" she asked.

"You mean the ones from Katie? Or Allie? Or whoever?"

"Let me tell her," Maureen begged.

Kayla heaved a sigh. "Fine, go ahead. You always get the good parts."

Maureen grinned. "Better idea. We'll act it out. You be Grandpa."

Kayla grabbed Maureen's hand and gave it a

rough shake. "Excellent performance, young man," she said in a low, gruff voice.

"Dude, thanks, Grandpa," Maureen said, trying her best to sound as airheaded as Anoop.

Kayla gave Maureen a stiff pat on the back. "Did you get the flowers I sent?"

Maureen batted her eyes. "They were bee-you-tee-ful!"

It was too awesome to be true. "His *grandpa* sent him those flowers?" I could barely choke out the words. It's kind of hard to have a conversation when you're laughing so hard it feels like you might spit out a vital organ.

Once we'd all calmed down, I dragged Maureen and Kayla over so they could meet my family, and my parents did their best not to embarrass me. (Alana, on the other hand, did everything she could think of to embarrass me. But that's what little sisters are for.)

When Alana finished telling the story of how I once threw up while battling flying monkeys in *The Wizard of Oz,* Maureen checked her watch. "We should probably head to the cast party soon," she said.

"Just one minute, girls," Great-aunt Silva said. "I want you to meet a friend of mine." Her arm shot into the air and she waved frantically until a thin man with a wispy black mustache appeared by her side.

"Giles Standish," he said, shaking hands with each of us. "Pleased to make your acquaintance. Silva's been gushing about her great-niece for years — I just had to meet her myself."

"Mr. Standish works with the national tour of *Les Miserables*," Great-aunt Silva explained. Kayla's eyes widened. Maureen gulped. "He's only in town for a couple days, but I told him he just *had* to come to the performance."

"And it was the right decision," Mr. Standish said. "You ladies put on a stellar show. Especially you," he told Maureen.

"Really?" Maureen asked in a tight, nervous voice. I could almost hear her heart pounding. "You really thought I was good?"

"Undoubtedly. That one song, 'Fang Through My Heart'? Remarkable voice for a girl your age. Even through the werewolf mask."

Maureen and I turned to each other at the same moment. She pressed her lips together, and a tiny shudder passed through her. Then she drew in a deep breath and stood up straighter. "Actually, Mr. Standish, that wasn't me," she said. "Ruby sang that one in my place."

"Oh." Mr. Standish cleared his throat. "Well, uh, yes. You were, of course, very good in the rest of it, as well. Very good. I — uh. Yes." He glanced over our heads. "I think I see someone over there I recognize, so if you'll excuse me . . . Ruby, say good-bye before you leave, all right?"

I nodded, pretty sure there wasn't anyone he recognized. He just wanted to get away from the big pile of awkward that he'd dumped on us.

"Thanks," I told Maureen, once he left. "You didn't have to do that."

"Of course I did," she replied.

"No," Kayla said, sounding surprised. "You really didn't. You could have just let him believe that it was you. But you didn't."

Maureen shrugged. "No big deal," she said, and I could tell she was trying really hard to pretend it was true.

I couldn't help it. I gave her a hug. "It's a big deal to me."

While everyone's families wandered around and introduced themselves, Kayla, Maureen, and I chattered excitedly about our plans for eighth grade. We would totally rule the drama club, we decided. We would force the principal to get us a new director, one who actually knew what she was doing. We would pick the show *we* wanted to do — something by Sondheim (Kayla's idea) or maybe Andrew Lloyd Webber (Kayla's nightmare). We would be unstoppable.

But first, we would hit the cast party.

"Don't forget, you're supposed to go talk to that Standish guy," Kayla said, pushing me in his direction as we headed for the door.

Giles Standish was waiting with my family and Great-aunt Silva, staring at his watch. He brightened when he saw me approaching. "Finally!" he said. "Look, I have to run out, so your family can pass along the details. The upshot is that we've got an opening on the tour, and we'd love to have you come in tomorrow and read for Eponine."

"Is it just because of that solo?" I asked, feeling terrible that I'd stolen Maureen's big shot.

Mr. Standish shook his head. "Are you kidding? Silva's been talking you up for years. If you're even *half* as good as she says, the part is yours. I gave your parents the time and place — all you need to do is show up and sing. If you get the part, rehearsals start Sunday. The show plays in LA for the next couple months, then leaves on a sixteen-city tour. Next stop, Las Vegas!"

I was frozen. And by the time I got myself unstuck enough to actually *say* something, he was gone.

Everyone stared at me. Great-aunt Silva looked overjoyed. My parents looked proud. Alana just looked down at her new soccer cleats. I spotted Kayla and Maureen over by the door, giggling as they reenacted the spectacular tumble Anoop had taken in the second act.

"Your father and I have talked it over," my mom said. "And if the audition goes well, you can take the part."

"But I thought you wanted me to stay at home." Why am I trying to talk them out of this? I thought.

"The show doesn't leave town until June," Mom said, "so you could finish out the school year. LA isn't that far of a drive — we can work something out."

"And we've seen how important this is to you," Dad added. "We want to support you, if this is what you really want."

But what *did* I want?

For the first time in a long time — maybe in my entire life — I had no idea.

Chapter 12

Diva Rule #12: *"You have got to discover you, what you do, and trust it."*
— Barbara Streisand
(star of *Funny Girl*)

"If you want to go, you should just go," Alana said.

"Well, maybe I do want to go," I said.

Alana shrugged, like she couldn't care less. "So do it."

"Maybe I will." If she was going to pretend she didn't care, I could do the same.

"Good."

"Good."

"So just do it," she said, rolling her eyes. "Go."

So I did.

But I didn't go alone.

"Remind me again what I'm doing here?" Kayla complained, slouching against the metal bleachers.

"Boring yourself to death?" Maureen suggested, pulling one of her earbuds out just long enough to respond. "I know that's what I'm doing." She stuck the earbud back in and turned up her music. Down on the field, the soccer ball soared out of bounds, and everyone around us started cheering. I had no idea why.

"It's not so bad," I shouted over the crowd. Kayla and Maureen looked at me like I was crazy.

"Okay, it's bad," I admitted as one of the coaches called yet another time-out. It felt like we'd been there for hours. According to the game clock, only ten minutes had passed. "But Alana really wanted me to see her play, even if she wouldn't admit it. Thanks for coming along."

"Well, you did bribe us," Maureen reminded me, waving one of the chocolate-chip cookies I baked.

Somewhere else, not so very far away, a bunch of girls were lining up for an audition. They were clutching their headshots, practicing their lines, crossing their fingers, making deals with the universe. And by the end of the day, one of them would be going home with what she wanted most in the world: the part.

The part that could have been mine.

"We're proud of you," my parents had said.

"You should go for it," Kayla and Maureen said.

"I knew you'd be back on top!" Great-aunt Silva said.

"If it's want you want . . ." Alana said.

And it *was* what I wanted — but for the first time, it wasn't the only thing. I wanted to run the drama club with Maureen and Kayla, even if it meant listening to their never-ending bickering. I wanted to eat Saturday morning pancakes with my parents, even if it meant doing the dishes. I wanted to get to know my sister again, even if it meant sitting through an incredibly long, boring soccer game that I was pretty sure would *never* end.

Alana ran back and forth across the field, until she finally got possession of the ball and gave it a mighty kick. I whooped and jumped to my feet as it flew straight into the net.

I still didn't get why anyone would voluntarily spend their afternoon chasing a ball around a field — and I *really* didn't get why anyone would want to watch them do it. But I had to admit, Alana was pretty good.

"How come you always get to be Nathan Detroit?" Kayla complained as Maureen began to sing along to the *Guys and Dolls* soundtrack.

(There are plenty of parts for girls in that show, but we all agreed that the only *good* parts were Nathan Detroit and Sky Masterson. Just one problem: Two of them. Three of us.)

"Um, because *I'm* the one who can sing?" Maureen pointed out.

"Ruby can sing," Kayla argued.

"That's why Ruby gets to be Sky Masterson," Maureen said.

"So what does that leave for me?" Kayla asked. "The horse?"

Maureen grinned. "If the horseshoe fits!"

"Compromise?" I suggested quickly. "How about we all sing all the parts?"

They both looked at me in horror. "That's totally unprofessional!" Kayla exclaimed.

"Yeah, what kind of practice is that?" Maureen teased. "You may be all about singing for the love of singing these days, or whatever, but *some* of us are still looking out for our futures."

Maureen was wrong.

Sure, I decided to try being a "normal" middle school kid for a while. (Not that there's anything "normal" about life when Maureen and Kayla are around — which is just the way I like it.) But I'm just as sure about my future as I've ever been. I *know* I'm destined for a bright, glittering life as a Broadway star. I'm destined for the spotlight. My name will be twenty feet high, in neon lights.

That's my future, I'm sure of it.

But now I'm sure of something else, too: The future can wait.

LYRICS TO "ZOMBIE DANCE PARTY"

Hear that sound, it's getting close,
A thousand shuffling feet?
The walking dead have come to town
For a Zombie Dance Party!

All we need are brains, sweet brains
And we're coming after yours.
You can try to run, that's half the fun
Of the Zombie Dance Party!

We're not very fast, or very smart
Be we've got a big head start.

So look out world, it's time to eat,
You call 'em "brains" — we call it "meat"!

It's a Zombie Dance Party!
A Zombie Dance Party!

read them all!

Accidentally
Fabulous

Accidentally
Famous

Accidentally
Fooled

How to Be a Girly Girl
in Just Ten Days

Miss Popularity

Making Waves

Totally Crushed

Callie for President

Another Candy Apple book . . .
just for you.

JUICY GOSSIP

by Erin Downing

Jenna Sampson, perfectly normal seventh grader and editor of the school newpaper, is mortified. Her parents are opening a superembarrassing juice bar at the mall. Jenna has to work there . . . *and* wear a ridiculous uniform. She's pretty sure her life can't get worse, until she finds out that the school paper might shut down.

But the gossip Jenna overhears from the juice bar is totally newsworthy, which gives her a great idea. A gossip column could be a huge hit and save the paper — or cause a ton of trouble!